A bullet snapped away a fragment of the collar of Raider's leather jacket. Raider twisted in the saddle, hauled his Remington from his holster, and was already pulling back on the hammer when his eyes located the telltale wisp of smoke.

An instant later the lead horseman lay in a heap on the ground. Raider beamed at the crowd of shocked faces benevolently:

"With me, you gotta make your first bullet count . . ."

Other books by
J. D. HARDIN

J. D. HARDIN

HOMESTEADER'S
REVENGE

BERKLEY BOOKS, NEW YORK

HOMESTEADER'S REVENGE

A Berkley Book/published by arrangement with
the author

PRINTING HISTORY
Berkley edition/October 1984

ISBN: 0-425-07381-5

A BERKLEY BOOK® TM 757,375
Berkley Books are published by The Berkley Publishing Group,
200 Madison Avenue, New York, New York 10016.
The name "BERKLEY" and the stylized "B"
with design are trademarks belonging to
Berkley Publishing Corporation.
PRINTED IN THE UNITED STATES OF AMERICA

HOMESTEADER'S
REVENGE

CHAPTER ONE

Willie McPhee rode with the miners on the trail down from
the high Sierra Nevada. This was his first assignment as a
Pinkerton operative in the field. His job was to escort the
miners with their nuggets and dust as far as Devil's Bowl,
a bottomless dark blue mountain lake that had pine, larch,
and spruce growing down its steep slopes to the edge of the
ice-cold water. The trail led west from there down into the
town of Sutter Creek, but another Pinkerton operative took
over from him at the lake for the most dangerous part of
the journey. This man was hard-bitten, experienced. Willie
wanted to make an impression on him by delivering the
miners safely into his hands. Then his job was done. From
Sutter Creek the miners would go to Sacramento, and from
there to San Francisco, where they would lose all their gold
anyway to whores, gamblers, and barkeeps. But that was
none of Willie's business. His concern was that the miners
didn't lose their gold along the way before they had a chance
to waste it in the big-city fleshpots.

He rode a powerful bay gelding in top condition, and

the big horse nonchalantly eased his way along the narrow, winding trail, hardly bothering with the nags on which the miners rode. Willie held his Winchester .44–.40 rifle, with its second rear sight for greater aiming accuracy, cross-wise on top of the saddle, and he looked up among the dark tree trunks as he rode. He checked every bluff and outcrop for marksmen, scanned the wilderness for any sign of movement, for a glint of metal, a telltale patch of colored cloth. . . . There was nothing. Apart from himself and the miners, there might not be another living soul in California.

Things were so wild and lonesome this high in the Sierra, they had met no one on the trail for days. Yet that was what the other miners had said—the few who had survived after being robbed. Their stories were all the same. They had been set upon by seven gunslingers—some said nine—in the middle of nowhere. Each time the thieves shot some of the miners without provocation just to frighten the others. Anyone slow to obey them, even out of fear or stupidity, got a lead slug in the gut.

The Sierra miners got to talking. Some said it was the assayers who sold the information to the holdup men on who was carrying gold. One drunk miner killed an assayer in a saloon after claiming the assayer was getting a percentage of the stolen gold. A federal marshal arrived to question the assayers. So far as they were concerned, this was the last straw. They hired Pinkertons to protect their reputations by protecting the miners. At least no one could say now that the assayers were part of the plot. When Pinkertons were set loose, they couldn't be reined in just because someone didn't like what they were turning up.

So far three bandits had died, all lone operators who had drifted in to grab a piece of the action, easy money with low risk, as they thought. Willie had blasted away one of them, the second Pinkerton the other two. This had been the first man Willie had killed, and he had been so slow to do it, he had nearly gotten killed himself instead.

But that had been ten days ago, and Willie had long since gotten over his upset at shooting the man. Now he was riding tall in the saddle, the metal of the Winchester barrel cold against his hands in the October mountain air. The sky was leaden and windless, and things had a sullen, silent look.

The miners were happy and talkative. They were heading down to winter quarters, and it would be March, April, or even May before the snows would have melted and the meltwaters subsided enough for them to resume their search for precious metals. By that time, all their hopes and illusions would be fully restored, and they would return to the mountains as naive as they had been on their first prospecting trip. Willie liked the miners. They were carefree and cheerful for the most part, and a little hardship and danger didn't get them to complaining like it did other folks.

But Willie had to admit that miners were kind of dumb. At least these ones were. Else, why would they feel so confident about putting their lives under the protection of a nineteen-year-old like himself who had never shot a gun at anything bigger than a rabbit till ten days ago? All that these miners seemed able to see was that he was a Pinkerton, so they must be safe if he was along. That was crazy, Willie felt the urge to tell them. He was just as scared of gunslingers as they were. And he probably wasn't half as handy with a gun as most of them, in spite of his intensive Pinkerton training. But they believed in him, Willie could see that. And seeing they believed in him, he started to believe in himself. Not too much. But enough to ride tall in the saddle and squint into the hard dull light to look for movements among the tree trunks. With his Remington .44-.40 held crosswise on the saddle, its gunmetal chilling to the touch...

On many parts of the trail there wasn't much any man could do except ride along hoping for the best, duck bullets if they came, and fire back at what he saw. Apart from some scares—a deer crashing through the undergrowth, a mountain lion attracted by the smell of horse—they had passed through all the danger spots without incident.

"Getting kind of cold up here this time of year," Willie said to one of the miners, "these drygulching critters can

probably find some easier form of work down in the towns
and cities. I'd hate to have to freeze my butt waiting around
for someone to come along this lonesome trail."

"A man will do a lot for a free helping of gold," the
miner replied abruptly. "You keep a weather eye out as we
come down to Devil's Bowl, young man. It warn't far from
the lake they put a finish to old Tucson Dan, God rest his
soul."

"I know the place," Willie said. "You ain't going to have
no trouble so long as you have me with you."

The grizzled miner looked at him in a funny way. He
even kind of smiled. Maybe he's laughing at me, Willie
thought.

Willie added, "Of course if we hit trouble, I could always
use your help."

"Reckon so."

They let it go at that.

They hit trouble soon after. They were moving through
a notch cut in a ridge by a stream, where the pines grew
huge on the slopes. Some monster trunks lay toppled after
their roots could no longer anchor their enormous bulk in
the shallow soil. Two men with rifles stood atop one of
these trunks. Only a trickle of water ran among the bleached
boulders in the streambed.

"You heading on down to Sutter Creek?" one of the two
men hollered.

The miners said nothing in reply, and Willie McPhee
suddenly realized they were waiting for him to say something.

"Mebbe so," he called back.

Willie reckoned they had seventy yards between them—
an easy shot with a rifle, just within range for a revolver.
These men could be anybody. They weren't pointing their
guns at him, and he wasn't waving his Winchester at them.
Just eyeing each other. Looking one another over. Real
careful. A man had to be out here. Even if he wasn't carrying
dust and nuggets.

"Git off them horses!" one of the men bawled.

"Right now!" the other yelled, bringing his rifle to bear. There could be no doubt in anyone's mind at this point.

Willie McPhee swung the long barrel of his .44-.40 from its crosswise position on the saddle so that it stuck out forward of his horse's nose; he fired from the hip and levered another bullet into the chamber.

The bandit who had spoken second, and leveled his rifle first, doubled over without getting to fire a shot. He wobbled on the huge pine trunk, lost his balance, and flopped on the ground.

Willie couldn't help thinking: That makes two.

It wasn't going to be that easy. Willie felt his horse rear up and then collapse under him. The bay gelding whinnied piteously as he went down. Willie stepped off his sinking mount as a second rifle bullet hit the brim of his Stetson and tore the hat from his head. The two shots came from behind some rocks a way up one of the slopes of the notch.

Willie dove for cover. The miners he was escorting jumped from their saddles and scattered among rocks and behind tree trunks as bullets spattered about them like hailstones. The thunder of rifles echoed and re-echoed off rock faces, and in pauses in the shooting could be heard still reverberating in steep-walled distant valleys.

"Everybody all right?" Willie yelled from behind his rock.

The miners called back, identifying themselves. By some miracle, none had been hit. Two of the horses were down and the rest had bolted. The miners held onto their guns and onto their gold, which they carried in buckskin belts.

They were taking fire from both sides of the notch, and it was all they could do to find cover that protected them from both directions. They were pinned down and could not fire back without exposing their backs to riflemen behind them.

"Throw down your guns and walk out into the open," a voice called to them. "We won't shoot."

"I think we should do as he says," one miner said to the others.

"You're a fool to think they won't blow your brains out," Willie said. "We killed one of their buddies. They'll want vengeance for that."

"*You* killed one of them, not us," the miner retorted.

"You think they'll give a damn about which of us did it?" Willie asked scornfully in the next break in the shooting. "They been killing miners who done nothing to them. You think they'll let you go after they kill me?"

The miner was silent.

Willie went on, "They were too cocksure in bushwhacking us here. Things have always gone smooth and easy for them before. This time one of them gets killed for being slow and careless. Those boys ain't too happy now. They're going to try to wipe us out, just to show who runs this show. But they're hurtin'. If we can nail another of them, they'll quit on us and go away to lick their wounds. We just ain't worth it to them. Best thing any of us can do right now is bag ourselves one more of them rat-assed critters."

"Willie, maybe if you left off talking and stuck your head up to do some shooting, we'd take more account of what you think we ought to do."

"Come on, Willie. Give 'em hell, boy!"

Willie raised his head to aim a shot with his Winchester and nearly had it blown off by three slugs from three different directions.

"Shit," he whispered hoarsely and huddled close as he could get to the ground while more bullets whistled above the rocks behind which he cowered. He could hear the miners cursing and taunting him while they too kept their heads down out of sight.

Willie heard rapid revolver shots followed by a howl of pain. He peered over the top of the rocks again. The gunslinger who had stood on the fallen tree with the man he had shot now lay on the ground beside his comrade, equally still. Then Willie saw a man zigzag up through the pines, making his way toward some of the riflemen, pinning them down. The riflemen shot at this new attacker, who returned their fire with a carbine as he advanced on them through the pines.

Willie emptied his Winchester on the riflemen, drawing some of their fire and interfering with their defense against the lone intruder. Several of the more courageous miners covered Willie's back, firing on the bandits on the opposite side of the notch.

He never knew whether it was one of his own bullets or a bullet from the stranger's carbine that scored the next hit. One of the bushwhackers suddenly stood erect, arms outstretched, his rifle fallen, and pitched slowly forward. One of the miners got lucky and hit one of the two riflemen on the far slope of the notch. He only winged him, but the second rifleman with him gave up the fight to help his buddy get away. The miners now all turned on the two remaining bandits still fighting from behind some rocks more than a hundred feet up the slope. Their mysterious rescuer had disappeared—only to reappear behind the two bandits. He walked them down, carbine blazing, then threw his empty weapon to one side and blasted six deadly shots from his revolver into their crouching bodies. Every shot counted. Willie could see the bodies of the men jerk spasmodically as the slugs hit them and then roll away lifeless as the gunfire stopped.

The newcomer went back to pick up his carbine, reloading his revolver as he went. It was only after he stepped over the bandits' corpses and came down toward them through the trees that Willie McPhee and the miners got their first good look at him.

He was a big man, six foot two, with broad shoulders and an easy way of walking. Beneath his black Stetson, he had coal-black eyes and a big black mustache. His skin was tanned and weather-beaten, his denims were tattered and worn, his black leather jacket beat up. Considering his size, he walked fairly silently through the trees in calfskin Middleton boots. The carbine was a .30-.30 Model 94 Winchester, and a Remington .44 was slung in the holster on his right hip.

"Raider!" Willie called out in recognition.

"I thought I might walk up to meet you," Raider said gruffly. He nodded shortly in the direction of the miners. "We should be getting on down to the lake before dark sets in. We can walk it easy from here. I'll put you men to fishing for supper while I go catch your horses."

The miners were at first suspicious of this rough, tough hombre till they learned from Willie he was the Pinkerton that would escort them as far as Sutter Creek. Raider had no trouble finding their horses where they had come down to drink and graze by the edge of the lake. He had spare horses to replace the two that had been killed. While the miners unpacked their bedding, Raider heated up a pot of precooked beans and fried trout in deer fat in a pan over the campfire.

No one said much about the shoot-out. After they had eaten, the miners crawled into their bedding about the fire and shivered in the autumn chill. Willie McPhee scribbled feverishly beneath a hurricane lamp. A few large flakes of snow drifted down slowly in the yellow lamplight.

"Did you mention me in your report, Willie?" Raider asked.

"Sure, Raider. I'm describing it just like it happened. You saved our hides."

"That's not what I mean. Just put in your report that I'm too busy or whatever to make my report, and say that yours will have to do for both of us."

Willie's eyes lit up with indignation. "But that's against the rules!"

"Who made the rules, Willie?"

"Allan Pinkerton."

Raider nodded. "Now tell me who made the world."

"God."

Raider grinned. "I thought you was going to say Allan Pinkerton."

• • •

Allan Pinkerton shifted his bulk in the leather chair behind the large walnut desk in his Chicago office. "I'll be perfectly frank with ye, Heron," he said in his strong Scottish burr. "Ye're the only man I still speak to who ever upped and left me."

Paul Heron tried not to smile, for he knew that the founder of the Pinkerton National Detective Agency was devoid of a sense of humor. Heron composed his florid jowls into a concentrated, serious expression, folded his fat pink fingers across his expansive belly, and kept his mouth shut.

The big Scotsman continued, "I don't like to train a man so others can have the benefit of my effort. But it's not only that. I sense an element of disloyalty in a man who leaves my force in order to carry on detective work elsewhere. I know what ye've a mind to say, Heron, that ye've never worked in competition with the Pinkertons and that furthermore ye've steered a fair amount of work our way since ye've left us. I appreciate that. But ye're not a man I'd trust again. That said and understood between us, Heron, what is it ye've come to see me about that a telegram wouldn't have taken care of just as well?"

Paul Heron realized that his old boss's fear was that he had come to ask for his old job back. Well, if that had been the case, he had just received his answer before he ever got to put the question. Heron respected Pinkerton for things like that. The founder of the detective agency might often be a self-important bore, but he was always outspokenly honest—and hang the consequences. Many men besides Paul Heron had a kind of unwilling liking for Allan Pinkerton because of his qualities.

"I'm on my way to California and I'll need a couple of your operatives," Heron said. "Good men, because it looks like a nasty job and I've no clear picture of what to expect."

Pinkerton raised his bushy eyebrows. "California? I thought ye were married and settled down in that railroad detective job in Ohio."

"I was till I accepted my new position as security chief with the Napa Valley Railroad Company."

Pinkerton snorted. "I never heard of it."

"It's a small railroad serving the Napa Valley, north of San Francisco. It's funded locally, not owned by one of the big railroads."

"It'll never last then."

"Maybe so, Mr. Pinkerton. I'll take a chance on that. Anyway trains are being stopped and robbed and railroad men had been killed. They say a bunch of roughneck squatters are responsible."

"That's what you're leaving a safe job in Ohio to go out to?" Allan Pinkerton said. "Taking your wife and children to a wilderness like that?"

"They'll follow later after I've got settled. And it's not a wilderness, Mr. Pinkerton. By all accounts, the valley is just as fertile as anything in Illinois or Ohio. I have the urge to go west while I'm still young enough to do it."

Pinkerton looked him over clinically. "It will take some of the flab off you. Is this little railroad of yours good for the money if I hire out operatives to it?"

"You have my word on that, Mr. Pinkerton."

"I've already told ye, Heron, I don't trust ye." The Scotsman permitted himself a tight little smile to show the other man it was all right for him to laugh at this joke.

Paul Heron laughed.

"Doc Weatherbee is in San Francisco," Pinkerton said, fingering through a sheaf of schedules.

Heron's face broke into a genuine smile. "I'd sure like to have him along."

"And Raider's out in the foothills of the Sierra Nevada, east of Sacramento somewhere. Ye've worked with Raider, haven't ye?"

Heron nodded. "You're giving me your two best men."

"I suppose I am," Pinkerton said. "One problem is that Raider has a novice along with him on the job, a young man named Willie McPhee. It mightn't be bad experience for him to go along too up to this valley of yours."

"I'll take him."

Pinkerton looked up from his papers. "I'll have to charge ye full rate even though McPhee's not an experienced operative."

"You got it."

Pinkerton hemmed and hawed. Heron could see he was not done yet in demanding concessions. He knew Heron would give a lot to get Weatherbee and Raider.

"I can't rightly tell ye when those lads'll finish their jobs out there," Pinkerton said. "It might so happen ye'd have to give them a hand if ye got there before they had finished. Since I trained ye meself, I know ye'd be useful to them."

"I'll do what I can, Mr. Pinkerton."

"Of course, since ye're no longer a member of my agency, I couldn't pay ye anything."

"I understand, Mr. Pinkerton."

Doc Weatherbee ignored as much as he could the pistol barrel pressing against his left cheekbone. He said, "It is not one of my duties, sir, to check the contents of the cargo, simply to guard it."

Nate Williams held the pistol's handle. "Seems to me you done a lousy job of guarding the cargo then."

"I have done better," Doc conceded.

The two men stood on a wooden wharf in the early morning San Francisco fog. A big clipper with an overhanging bow, tall raked masts, and furled sails was barely visible tied to the dock only thirty feet away. The salty tang of the ocean was as heavy as the fog in the air. Bell buoys made ghostly chimes out on the bay, and the barks of sea lions were eerily loud in the shifting insubstantial palls of overwhelming fog.

"Load 'em up, lads," Nate Williams called to four men. "We'll find out what's in them casks soon enough. Whatever it is, t'will be worth our while."

As Williams continued to press the gun barrel against Doc's left cheekbone, without a tremor in his hand, one of the men backed up two big draft horses harnessed in a low-sided wagon. The men lowered the rear gate of the wagon and placed two long heavy timber planks at an easy angle from the ground up to the wagon's floor. After tipping the cargo barrels on their sides, where they were stacked on the wharf, they rolled them up the two planks onto the wagon, where they stood them on end again, close to each other so they could fit them all on. The barrels stood four feet high, and their wooden staves, held by three iron hoops, had a widest diameter of about three feet across the middle. They might contain anything, from rice to whiskey to bales of cloth, depending on where the clipper had sailed from. They had been unloaded the previous day and not picked up by their intended receiver.

"They got to be valuable if they put that damn Pinkerton Weatherbee there to guard 'em," Nate had told his pals after they had first spotted the barrels. "Remember him last week? He done Jervis out of all that Chinese silk."

"And the machine parts that Kelly and Lombardi almost got their hands on," another man complained.

"Weatherbee is making it hard for everyone scratching a living down here on the docks." Nate spat. "If this goes on, we'll all end up having to work for our supper."

That caused muffled laughter among the men as they passed in their wagon. Doc was plainly visible, striding back and forth by gaslight on the wharf. He was dressed in the latest big-city style, with no allowance for the surroundings he found himself in now. His pearl gray derby had a curly brim, his suit was of the finest-quality wool, his vest and shirt were silk, and he wore overgaiters. Doc flipped the glowing end of his cheroot over the wharf edge into the black slapping sea. Long wraithlike tongues of fog snaked in toward the land from out in the Pacific.

"Give the mist a chance to build, lads," Nate said, cracking the reins over the ample rumps of the two draft horses. "We'll come back in an hour to pay the doctor a visit."

They spent a pleasant sojourn in a waterside tavern that remained open all night for the convenience of men like Nate Williams. When the fog rolled like thick smoke outside the tavern doorway and deposited a coating of tiny water drops on all the windowpanes, Nate nodded to his men and swallowed down his dark rum spiked with ginger.

Doc Weatherbee was still walking to and fro near the barrels when they got there. Nate slipped off the wagon and crept along, invisible and silent, behind Doc as the latter kept an eye on the moving wagon and its occupants as best he could in the poor visibility. Before Doc knew what was happening to him, Nate had the gun barrel pressed to his left cheekbone.

When all the cargo barrels were loaded on the wagon, Nate said to Doc, "Climb up."

The two big draft horses pulled their burden through the early morning city streets. The first workers—bakers, vegetable vendors, fish sellers—were opening stores or setting up stalls. Oil and gas lamps were being lit inside houses by those early to rise. Nate held the pistol barrel snug against Doc's ribs lest he should get a sudden urge to leave his present company or call out to someone on the street.

The wagon pulled up to a warehouse next to a church not far from the docks. Two of the men climbed down to unlock and open the big double doors, and the wagon rolled inside.

"I've noticed this place," Doc told Nate, "when I was looking for your hideout."

"You thought it was part of the church?"

"Right."

Nate guffawed. "So does everyone else. Including the police."

Merchandise, half spilled out of cargo barrels, lay all about the spacious warehouse's ground floor. Apparently anything that could not be immediately sold off was just abandoned there. The men rolled three of the barrels down the planks to the warehouse floor and stood them on end again. Nate looked on expectantly as the men opened the tops of the barrels with mallets.

The top came off the first barrel to reveal an upside-down pair of large black boots with legs attached. The tops of the other two barrels were removed almost simultaneously. Two uniformed city patrolmen popped up waisthigh out of the confinement of the barrels.

One shouted, "Come out fast, men!"

The tops of the barrels still on the wagon immediately erupted and a cop rose out of each barrel except for the ones which had been placed upside down, whose ends were kicked by large black boots and thrashing legs.

One of the thieves turned to run, and four police revolvers spat flame in a roar made deafening by the high tin ceiling and bare brick walls of the warehouse. The thief splayed grotesquely on the floor, almost beneath the rearing hooves of the frightened draft horses. Red puncture marks on the body were entrance and exit wounds. Nate Williams dropped his pistol like it had grown searing hot in his hand. None of the other thieves looked as if they wanted to try their luck throwing lead either.

The policemen looked mean, cramped, out of breath, and anxious to use the big revolvers they leveled on the thieves. They looked none to friendly at Doc Weatherbee also, because it was he who had persuaded their lieutenant to put them through their ordeal in the barrels.

Doc thanked Nate Williams for the ride on his wagon, tipped his derby to the glowering sergeant, and headed for the street. Long experience had hardened Doc to the lack of gratitude on the part of others for his efforts in law enforcement.

The fog was beginning to thin out in the morning sunshine as Doc Weatherbee strolled along the city street. His allnight vigil on the wharf and his early morning endeavor had caused him to work up a good appetite. He stopped off first at the Western Union telegraph office and then found a clean refreshment place, where he ordered a fry of pork chops, eggs, and potatoes and eagerly sipped coffee about a quarter as strong as he liked.

Doc had noticed the girl as soon as he walked into the place. She was about twenty, sitting with two large garment bags—obviously all her possessions in the world—before a cup of cold coffee. Her light brown hair was pulled back tight from her face, very prim and proper, in a tight bun at the back of her head, and her face looked freshly washed and shiny. She had a determined mouth and bold blue eyes, and she kept her glances to herself. At least she did until Doc's food arrived. It must have been the aroma of the pork chops she couldn't resist. Doc was man enough to be amused by the fact that she was looking at his food instead of him. Without her noticing his doing it, Doc winked at the waiter, glanced at his plate, and then at the girl. When the waiter placed a loaded plate before her a few minutes later, she looked up in alarm and tried to explain. The waiter pointed at Doc and walked away. She blushed, looked uncertain for a moment, then picked up her knife and fork. She permitted Doc to join her at her table for coffee when she had finished eating.

"You're not going to keep your shape long, miss, putting away hearty breakfasts like that," Doc said teasingly.

"I won't have much trouble with my figure if I eat only once every two days," she responded quickly, well able to take care of herself in conversation with a stranger.

Doc shook his head in mock disapproval. "What modern young ladies will do these days to keep a fashionable figure . . . You eat only once every two days to stay slender?"

"I think you know very well I haven't a dollar to my name," the girl shot back with a glint in her eye. "And you're certainly in no position yourself to criticize any woman about her fondness for fashion."

Doc used his pearl gray derby to brush an imaginary speck of dust off his silk vest, which was canary yellow with scarlet fleurs-de-lis.

They both laughed, and the girl dropped her guard. She told him her name was Alice, she had just arrived from St. Louis, where she had been born, and hoped to find work as a cook in one of the rich men's houses on Nob Hill. Doc in turn told her he was a Pinkerton, had finished his assignment in San Francisco, and expected to be leaving the city later in the day. Since the Pinkerton National Detective Agency had paid for his hotel room through the end of October, she was welcome to live in it till then. No strings attached.

"I was warned about men like you," Alice said doubtfully. "How do I know you ain't some kind of white slaver and I'll never be heard of again?"

Doc showed her his Pinkerton identification papers and the telegram he had picked up from Western Union, telling him to contact Raider in Sutter Creek and then proceed to Napa City.

"I'll tell you what I plan to do, Alice," he said. "I've been out all night, so I aim to catch a few hours' sleep, then check the Western Union office to see if there's a response to my telegram to Raider. If he doesn't need me out in Sutter Creek, I'll go north to Napa City this afternoon. If he needs me in Sutter Creek, I'll go there. If I don't hear from him, I'll wait till tomorrow before I go out there."

"What do I do?"

Doc placed a ten-dollar gold piece on the table in front of her. "You can stay in another room or at another hotel for tonight if you have to."

She didn't pick up the gold piece. "Why are you doing this?"

Doc shrugged. "In my line of business, I have to do a lot of bad things to mostly bad people who deserve them. Every now and then I do something kind for someone who needs help to try to persuade myself I'm not a monster."

Alice laughed. "I believe you. I'll put my bags in your hotel room right away, if that's all right." She picked up the gold piece. "And I insist on paying for both our breakfasts."

At the hotel, Doc threw himself on the bed, exhausted. He talked with her awhile as she examined her new quarters with curiosity. Without realizing it, he drifted into a deep sleep.

Doc felt himself climb out of a dream, half wakened by pleasant sensations and half lulled back to sleep by the soothing feelings in his body. Excitement won out, and he became fully conscious to find his most treasured possession in Alice's mouth.

As he lay stretched on his back on the bed, she lay curled at his legs with her head on his belly. While he still slept, she had unbuckled his belt and unbuttoned his fly, hauled everything down to half-mast, and then used her fingers and lips to arouse his cock.

She kissed his lower belly repeatedly, letting his erect dick rub against her soft neck, as she gently massaged his balls in her cupped palm. She pulled on his pubic hair with her teeth and tongued the insides of his thighs.

She ran her tongue over and under the head of his cock, lapped on the length of his shaft, and kissed his balls. By now Doc was fully awake, eyes popping out of his head.

Circling his dick with her finger and thumb, she ran her hand up and down his member in time with her lips sucking the knob. Then she let his extended member sink deep in her throat, gasping wildly between its thrusts.

Just when Doc was on the point of shooting hot gism over her tonsils, she abandoned his dick, rolled on her back, hiked up her dress, and moaned, "Fuck me! Fuck me!"

Doc, half hog-tied with his pants about his ankles, rolled over and lay atop her. She parted her legs and raised her knees. He felt her fingers guide his throbbing cock into the warm moist slit of her sex.

He let the bulbous head pause inside the lips of her vulva, and felt the blind mouthing of her hungering cunt—and then its shuddering ecstasy as he pushed his powerful manhood into her damp aching void.

CHAPTER TWO

When Raider got to the Western Union office at Sutter Crook, there were two telegrams for him. The neat handwriting of the telegraph clerk reminded him of that of the teacher in his one-room country schoolhouse back in Arkansas. That old iron lady had sworn she would learn him to read and write if it killed them both, and it darn near had.

> Telegraph Doc Weatherbee in San Francisco to make contact before proceeding to Napa City, Calif. Client Paul Heron will accompany Weatherbee. McPhee to accompany you.
>
> Wagner

This was about as uninformative as the usual telegram from headquarters, but Raider always felt they made his telegrams a little extra uesless in revenge for his admittedly abrupt reports. The news that he was to work again with Paul Heron pleased him so much that he felt only a little irritated with having drawn Doc Weatherbee as a partner. However, his tolerance was short-lived. The second telegram read:

> My assignment successfully completed in San Francisco. I am instructed by Chicago to assist you in completion of yours, if completion not yet achieved. Unless I hear from you otherwise, I will meet you in Sutter Creek with all speed. I wired to Paul Heron at Cheyenne railroad stop. He will pick up next wire when his train gets to Sacramento and join us either at Sutter Creek or San Francisco."

Doc

Raider ground his teeth with rage. This was a typical Weatherbee. First the self-satisfied crap about assignments successfully completed on his part, along with an offer to help out a slower colleague. Then all the arrangements made for everybody without any consultation. Raider crumpled the telegraph form in a ball and angrily threw it in a corner of the office. Then he remembered his training and retrieved the paper, flattened it, and tore it into small unreadable pieces. This did not mellow his mood. Doc could go rot. Raider was damned if he was sending anyone telegrams about anything, whether it was yes, no, or maybe.

Still, he could look forward to seeing Paul Heron. Raider was not at all surprised Heron was making the move to California. Last time Raider had seen the ex-Pinkerton operative in Ohio, he had been overweight, bored, deskbound, and self-pitying. Raider could listen to a man bitching about his lot and in most cases sympathize with him—he himself did his own share of grouching and complaining. But somehow Paul had got on his nerves, and he had told Paul he was becoming a fat-assed office manager and too much of a butterball to be a real railroad detective anymore. Raider now hoped Paul hadn't taken what he had said too seriously. Raider certainly hoped his words had nothing to do with Paul throwing things over and coming out west. The last thing Raider needed was responsibility for something like that. He must have been drinking. Otherwise he'd never have said such things to Paul.

Worry over Willie McPhee had not done much to improve Raider's mood. When he had last parted with McPhee, at Devil's Bowl, snow had been falling in flurries—nothing to worry about but a signal to delaying miners of things to come. Two days later, with no warning, a blizzard hit the high Sierra, dumping two or three feet of snow which drifted to twelve feet in places. Then the weather cleared but stayed windy and mild, which made the snow impossible to travel over. The previous night there had been a deep frost, and by now the snow had had a chance to compact. As yet there was no word or sign of Willie McPhee.

Doc Weatherbee's telegram made up Raider's mind for him. Raider was damned if he was going to let Doc find him sitting on his ass in Sutter Creek wondering what had become of Willie. It had been agreed between him and Willie that Willie would take the last party of miners all the way down into Sutter Creek, without Raider coming out to meet them at the lake. Something had gone wrong somewhere. Raider was reasonably sure that all the bushwhackers had been taken care of for the moment. Any he hadn't chased off, the snow would. Which meant that McPhee and his party might be stuck in a drift somewhere. Or lost in the steep-sided valleys between the mountain folds. Damn, he thought, they couldn't be lost. All they had to do was keep walking west and downhill this side of the Sierra—it wasn't crazy and complicated like the Rockies.

Earlier in the day he had noticed an Indian at the edge of town selling long sheepskin coats, fur mitts and helmets, and snowshoes.

"What's my best way up to Devil's Bowl in snow?" Raider asked after buying his outfit. "Try to follow the trail?"

The Indian shook his head. "Don't go."

"I'm going."

The Indian pointed to a gap in the pines on a tall ridge.

"That way. Then you walk where the wind leaves little snow on the ground, you think. But maybe deep. You do not know."

Raider nodded. He had understood enough. Go any way he thought he wouldn't disappear into a snowdrift. But expect the worst. Good advice.

He strapped a sleeping roll on his back and hung his carbine from his right shoulder on a leather strap. He stuffed food in the pockets of the sheepskin coat, then decided to dump the food from one pocket in favor of a bottle of bourbon. At least he wouldn't have to carry water—there was enough of the shit frozen on the ground to float Noah's ark.

The icy wind lifted the powder snow and whipped it across Raider's face. Although no sun shone in the leaden sky, the snowfields were dazzlingly bright. He had to pull the hood of his fur helmet down over his face to protect his eyes from both the slashing wind and snow blindness. The long coat was warm though clumsy, and it kept his body heat trapped inside it. But his feet were so cold they had lost almost all feeling. His fingers inside the mitts were not much better—he knew he could not move his cold stiff fingers well enough to fire his carbine or revolver.

The snowshoes were the greatest disaster. He decided that such implements were never meant to be used by a man as big and heavy as he was, since he floundered and sank in the snow when he put them on. Raider knew well that snowshoes operated on the same principle as a bear's paws, and that a moving six-hundred-pound grizzly could cross the surface of a snowfield without breaking through it, whereas the pointed hooves of a fifty-pound deer would cause the animal to sink and founder. He trudged up the mountain slope, trying to keep to forest floors, where the snow was not deep and its depth was easy to gauge, and to the windward side of ascending ridges, where it was bitterly cold but swept down to the bare rock.

Raider cursed Willie McPhee. When he tired of that, he

cursed Doc Weatherbee. Then Allan Pinkerton. Between cursing them, he cursed himself. And when even that didn't keep his mind occupied, he thought of blistering hot days in Texas when the sweat ran into his eyes and stung them and big cactuses shimmered in the heat.

So long as he didn't think about what he was actually doing, about being cold and miserable, Raider found he could go on almost as if he were sleepwalking. He pushed forward on his numb feet and legs, working his fingers inside his mitts to keep their circulation going, squinting from the painful glare of the snow, keeping his nose tucked inside the high collar of his coat in order to breathe air heated by his body rather than the cold air outside, which was icy as mountain stream water.

Raider had spent the night at a miners' supply store in the foothills that rented small cabins by the night out back, each with its own wood-burning stove. At this time of year and in the spring, there was no shortage of emergency stop-overs at the place. Raider spoke with the men he met there. They were all coming down from the Sierra. He was the only one going up. They hadn't seen any sign of McPhee, and none of them knew what any of the other miners were doing, how many were still in the mountains, or who was where. None of them had come down by Devil's Bowl, even though that was the shortest route, because they had heard it was impassable.

Raider reckoned that if he left at dawn, he could trek to Devil's Bowl and return to his cabin at the supply store before dark. Right now, as he trudged through the snow-smothered wilderness, he wondered if he would be able to find the lake called Devil's Bowl, and failing to find it, whether he would be able to find his way back to that hot stove in the little log cabin, which seemed now like a happy memory from long, long ago.

Raider listened to the dry snow crunch under his feet as he climbed a steep slope alongside a pinewood. A movement in the trees caught his eye. He stopped and looked up hopefully. Seven timber wolves were pacing and watching him.

• • •

It took four locomotives to ram the Bucker snowplow through the drifts in the passes and canyons. The plow, a steel wedge with a boatlike prow superimposed on it, rode before the first locomotive and stood higher than it. The plow did a fine job on accumulations of snow on open level reaches. When the snow piled into heavy drifts or when the wheels lacked traction on an incline, the locomotives sometimes had to back up repeatedly to gain distance in order to build up speed to ramrod the plow through the snowbank. These impacts could be rough on passengers, especially when the train traveling at top speed came to a sudden shuddering halt against solid snow deep in a drift and they were thrown forward in the coaches, as steam spat explosively from the engine valves.

There were two schools of thought as to which was the less comfortable, even less dangerous, way to survive this. Some felt they were better off inside the coaches, protected from the elements, no matter what occurred. Others found greater safety in standing shivering knee-deep in a railside snowbank, while the iron horse plunged in combat with the drift.

Paul Heron supported both schools of thought. He hugely enjoyed being pitched about in the coaches and also standing on the sidelines cheering the engineers and firemen on. He was totally unaware that some of his fellow passengers found his enthusiasm insufferable. Certainly it can be hard to tolerate someone who seems not only to be immune to, but even to thrive upon, what others regard as discomfort or inconvenience. Paul of course was simply reliving some of his days as a railroad detective after he first left the Pinkertons, before he settled down into a managerial position in Ohio. He could name half a dozen of the best engineers on any main line and knew all the stories—such as how twelve locomotives had to be used to push a plow through thirty-foot drifts in the Sierra winter of 1867. Those were the days. . . .

"I'm not sure I should be coming to California," the man sitting next to Paul Heron in the train repeated.

"All I got to say," Heron told him, "is that if things don't work out for you there, it will probably be because of your own attitude."

Heron had tired of listening to the family's troubles in Boston, and he didn't want to hear a detailed description of the misfortunes they expected to befall them in California. People like them, if gold coins showered on them, would complain of being hit on the head. Some people's attitude was plain bad, whatever the circumstances. Paul was reminded of the old rhyme:

Two men looked out behind bars.

One saw mud, the other stars.

The man's wife rarely spoke, except to complain to her husband about the cold or the delays or the scenery. The kids were happy enough—if their parents' sourness didn't get to them, they'd make good Californians.

When the boy asked Paul, "Sir, you ever seen a real gunfighter out here?" he was glad to change the subject of conversation. The adults had already expressed a distaste for his train stories. To hell with them; he'd talk to the kid.

"Have I ever seen a real gunfighter?" Heron asked rhetorically and whistled. "The meanest baddest biggest guntotin' hombre in the whole West is a friend of mine. I remember one time he and me was in Texas. We was riding a train south, guarding a shipment of gold bullion to San Antone. Out in the dryland mesquite, a gang ripped a pair of rails out of the roadbed and eight of them waited there, armed to the teeth, sitting on their horses, knowing the train had to stop. Turned out later, after their bodies were identified, some of 'em had ridden at times with the James brothers."

The boy's eyes widened in wonder.

"Low-down thievin' murderin' critters, all of 'em," Heron

told him in a sinister tone. "No meaner scabs than these ever fell off a running sore on a whore's"—Paul remembered his juvenile audience—"I mean, on a steer's, eh, side. Anyway, you get the picture, kid. These were not decent upstanding citizens like your father and I. When the train stopped, they came to the locomotive cab, hauled the engineer and fireman out, then shot them just for fun. Sure as I'm sitting here, they blew them both apart, so they was just like two leaky old bags oozing stuff onto the dirt."

"Do we have to listen to this, Mr. Heron?" the boy's father inquired in his best Boston prig manner.

"Please, Daddy, let him," the kid cried.

Heron went on before the disgruntled parent had a chance to say anything else. "Then they started dragging passengers out of the coaches, kicking them on the rump so they'd move fast—but they weren't interested in robbing them. They knew the gold shipment was aboard a freight car and that they'd have a fight on their hands before they took it. They wanted to flush out the armed men among the passengers first and take their weapons in case they'd help the guards, which was me and this deadeye gunfighter name of Raider. Big man from Arkansas, big black mustache, covered with scars, like lightning with his gun. He'd tear your face off with a .44 slug soon as look at you, and you'd never know what hit you. Kind of man we had guardin' that gold."

"Go on," the boy said.

"Well, they cleared that whole train of everybody, caboose and all, 'cept for us two inside that boxcar with the gold bullion in strong wooden boxes. Raider was sitting on maybe a quarter million dollars of gold bars, twirling the chambers of his big six-shooter, calm as pondwater. I was scared so much I wanted to pee in my pants."

"Did you?" the boy asked seriously.

"Nearly."

"Mr. Heron..." This time it was the mother.

Paul ignored her. "Raider looked at me with his deep black eyes and said, 'Paul, you open that door and walk out there with your hands held high. Tell those varmints you're the only guard and they can have the gold, all you want is your life.' So I did as he said. I slid the door to one side a piece and waved my hat out the opening to see if they'd shoot. When they didn't, I showed myself and threw out my rifle and revolver. Then I jumped down and walked over to where the passengers stood. 'Who else is in there?' one of the train robbers shouted at me. 'I'm the only guard,' I said. 'You can have the gold, all I want is my life. Ain't no one else in there.' Then I kept walking, with my hands in the air, 'fore they thought to torture me or anything."

"Would they torture you?" the kid asked.

"Oh, sure. Pull out your fingernails, burn cigarette holes in your skin, all sorts of things. Didn't I tell you these were real badmen? So one of them, a mean-lookin' critter, maybe he was their leader, motions to the others to stay back, and he walks real careful up to the boxcar with the door slid open a little ways. He looks in. Then with his revolver held before him, he climbs in. They all wait. Nothing. Then two of the others say, 'He's picking the best stuff for himself,' and they follow him in. The others wait. Again, nothing. So they all run toward the boxcar, shouting, 'That gold's ours, too.' Raider brings down four of them with his carbine. But the fifth and last of them draws a bead on Raider while he's shooting the others and is just about to squeeze the trigger of his revolver when I . . ." Heron paused for breath.

"What did you do?" the boy asked urgently.

"I reached in my right boot and drew out my Colt New Line Pocket .41—little gun had a two and a quarter inch barrel—and fanned off two shots into the critter's back before he could shoot my comrade. One of those bullets snapped his spine in two like you'd kill a rattler with a stick."

The small boy looked at the fat middle-aged storyteller in unconcealed disbelief. "You expect me to believe that, mister?"

To prove his point, and sensing he could be rude to this stranger his parents disliked and go unpunished, the youngster dove his hand into Heron's right boot. His little hand came out holding a worn Pocket .41. The kid looked mighty impressed.

His mother screamed.

The Indian did a playful imitation of a big man trying on a sheepskin coat.

"That's Raider," Doc Weatherbee confirmed, laughing.

Paul Heron nodded in agreement. He had picked up Doc's telegram at Sacramento and come to meet him at Sutter Creek. Since Doc had not heard from Raider, he had come to help. If another man had disappeared after picking up his telegram and not replying to it, Doc would have been worried. With Raider, he knew the rules were different. Raider's great weakness was that he could never blend into his surroundings—both his appearance and behavior were usually striking, when not bizarre. People tended not to forget him easily. Which made him easy to find.

This Indian proved that point. He stretched a finger toward the gap in the pine trees on the distant ridge where he had directed Raider.

"Devil's Bowl. I said not go there. Big crazy man said he go. He go."

The Indian got to sell two more sheepskin coats, fur mitts and helmets, and snowshoe pairs. Outside town Doc and Paul ran into a group who had met Raider at the cabins behind the miners' supply store.

"He set out for Devil's Bowl at first light. Said he would be back before dark," one man told them. "He didn't come back."

"We warned him," another said.

"You bet we did."

"He went anyway. Never saw the fella again."

"Won't neither. He's buried in a drift somewheres. They'll find him fresh as a daisy come spring melt. Seen it myself. You'd think he'd been only hours dead."

Conditions were easier for Doc and Paul than they had been for Raider. The wind had died down, yet the temperature stayed low, with the result that the snow was more easily passable. Doc showed Paul the best technique to use with snowshoes, and they made good time across areas they otherwise would have had circle. At the miners' supply store, where they took a cabin for the night, there was still no word of Raider.

"All the others were coming down from the mountains and he was going up," the owner explained in exasperation. "I tried to stop him. So did the others. But he wasn't the kind that's easy to stop—excepting you happened to be a grizzly bear or an elephant."

Doc nodded. "Even then I wouldn't be sure."

Doc and Paul set out before dawn the next day.

"You got any next of kin you want me to inform?" the store owner asked as they left.

Doc turned to him. "You got any bottles of good bourbon left?"

The man looked puzzled. "A few. Why?"

"Keep them for us."

Doc Weatherbee could hear the hoarse rasping of Paul Heron's breath as he trailed behind over the snowfields. He waited for the pudgy, overweight man to catch up.

Doc took one look at him and had to laugh. "How can you manage to work up such a sweat in this frigid air?"

Paul grinned rufully. "I was thinking the same thing myself. It's so godawful cold, the drops of perspiration are turning into little balls of ice on my skin. I'm not kidding." He sank down on the snow for a rest, panting. "You remember me when I was lean and fit, eh, Doc?"

"Sure. That's not so long ago."

"I know that." Heron shook his head. "The fitter and tougher you are, the heavier you fall into the soft life. Don't never let your body go, Doc."

Doc shrugged. "Never for more than a day or two at a time anyway."

"I wasn't counting a bit of heavy recreation now and then. We all need that. You know, this job in California's either going to shape me up or kill me."

"Is that why you came?" Doc asked.

"That's right. No matter what happens to me out here in California, it's better than a slow death in Ohio. I felt I was slowly suffocating on that job. I was even getting around to blaming my wife and kids for how I felt. Already I see it's nothing to do with them. I miss them. I may look awful right now, but I'm feeling great for the first time in quite a while. If this kills me, I'll die happy." He got to his feet and punched Doc playfully with a fur mitt. "Let's go find that big clown Raider so we can curse him out for causing us to trek way to hell up into the mountains to save his useless ass."

They plodded onward toward Devil's Bowl until they came to huge slopes angling steeply upward, covered with virgin snow. They made their way along the base of the slopes, looking for tracks upward.

"It's possible the wind has completely covered his tracks with blown snow, even though it hasn't snowed again since Raider left," Doc said. "Anyway, let's make a complete survey down here where the going's relatively easy, before we start to climb farther."

Paul made no objection to delaying their ascent.

The survey paid off. They found a set of prints going down into a valley to the southwest.

"It may not be Raider," Doc said. "But this is the only lead we got. Let's follow."

After a distance they saw from the tracks that their maker had donned snowshoes at this point to cross a broad basin of deep snow. Doc and Paul followed suit. The prints of the snowshoes became irregular and erratic, and in a few places depressions in the snow indicated that the wearer of the snowshoes had fallen. Then they found a broken snowshoe, snapped in half. They could tell by the bindings that it was made by the same Indian craftsman who had made their own.

"It's Raider!" Doc yelled. "He got in a rage with the snowshoes and broke this one in half."

"Where's the other one?" Paul asked.

"He probably flung it away as far as he could."

Paul laughed. "Sure sounds like Raider all right."

Their pace quickened now. They felt new energy for their search and were openly glad they didn't have to climb higher in the Sierra. After an hour, though, they had lost their initial feeling of exhilaration and were becoming irritated at these silent footsteps that led on and on.

Then Doc thought he heard a sound. At first he considered that it must be in his mind. But it continued, insistent.

"You hear anything?" he asked Paul.

"Yeah." Paul pointed to their right. "From over there."

"Fiddle music from under a snowbank?" Doc was being careful.

"You hear that too?" Paul asked with obvious relief.

The footprints went past the snowbank a way and then suddenly turned to the right as if Raider, when he had walked by, had heard the fiddle at this point and headed toward it. Doc and Paul followed the tracks.

Ma Early was never one to let the cupboard go bare. Late each summer she stocked enough booze to last till the following summer. She never forgot the time when ten miners had been stranded by raging blizzards for six weeks at her place. All ten miners had had a rich season, and they bought her booze and her girls night and day till they left a month and a half later, exhausted and considerably poorer than they had come in. Her present crowd of refugees was not in that class, but they were not so bad either. They had run through a fair amount of whiskey and girls in the last few days. Her big worry now was that one of them would wake sober enough to realize it had stopped snowing and that any of them steady enough to walk could make it down to Sutter Creek and to the outside world. She knew all the girls—except Tessie, who was too dumb—intended to skip to San Francisco for the winter first chance they got. They'd leave with the men, and she mightn't see hardly a soul till next March or April.

Ma Early shifted her enormous bulk, and the wickerwork armchair beneath her crackled explosively. She put a match to the bowl of her pipe and belched out a puff of blue smoke that rose slowly to mix with the layers of smoke beneath the blackened ceiling. Ma knew about music, vice, and booze. One thing she wanted no part of was gambling. It got folks killed. And besides, serious gamblers went easy on whiskey, women, and fiddlers, since they had to keep their heads clear. Blind Bob Thompson was hitting nice form with his bow, and she was hoping the fiddler was already marooned for the winter, being unable to see— though she hadn't noticed his lack of sight interfering in anything he wanted to do so far.

Her mind was occupied with these thoughts when the door was pushed open and two newcomers entered along with a draft of freezing air.

As soon as he walked in, Doc Weatherbee saw Raider. He would have been hard to miss. He was dancing to the fiddle music with one of Ma Early's girls on top of a table. He waved casually to Doc when he saw him but jumped down to the floor when he spotted Paul Heron. He shook Paul's hand.

"Did you find Willie McPhee?" Doc asked in a businesslike tone.

Raider looked at him truculently before answering, "Over there." He jerked his thumb over his right shoulder.

A thin young man was sleeping with his face on a table.

"Is he all right?" Doc asked.

Raider grinned and shook his head. "He's going to feel sick as a dog when he comes down off this. He'd been here, along with his party of miners, for three days when I arrived. Come on over and meet Ma Early."

Practical as always, Doc realized they were going nowhere that day. He would try to move out tomorrow morning before the partying began. In the meantime, he might as well enjoy himself.

Doc created a sensation among the girls when he pulled off his long sheepskin coat and furs and emerged as a smart city gent, complete with derby and overgaiters, in the snow-bound wilderness. A red-haired cutie took his fancy.

"You take me with you outta here when you go?" she whispered seductively to him, her full sensual lips trembling with hope.

"You don't like this snow?"

She shuddered in her thin silk gown.

Doc then saw that her hair was dyed crimson rather than plain red and that it nearly matched the crimson of her lips and that of the corset she wore beneath the thin gown. Her breasts were bare beneath the silk, and so were her legs and bush.

"I'd be willing to pay my fare," she said, sweet as honey.

When she walked, her butt wiggled, and slits up the sides of her gown opened momentarily to reveal long shapely thighs and calves.

"Are you going to travel in that outfit?" Doc asked.

"I always dress for the occasion," she said. "And some-how I got the notion that you and I were not quite ready yet to hit the road. I got a pair of snow-white sheets on a bed in the back room, if you want to check out what sort of partners we'll turn out to be on the trail. I hear that sort of thing's important."

"Very," Doc agreed gravely. "A check on our mutual compatability would be almost essential to the success of such a voyage."

She giggled. "It's a real pleasure to meet a highfalutin john."

Ida, for that was her name, looked a little shook after days—or weeks, or perhaps even months—of debauchery. Yet so far as Doc was concerned, there was nothing like tramping about in freezing snow all day to create a hunger in a man for warm flesh. She looked good to him.

He went with her to her back room, where he couldn't help but notice that the sheets on the bed were a lot less than snow-white. But Doc had other things on his mind than the frequency or quality of the laundering. Ida let enough of herself hang out to distract any red-blooded male.

And she enjoyed doing it. She strutted about the room in her heels, her robe open down the front, revealing her bare breasts above the red corset and her bush beneath it, which she had not dyed to match the rest. It was a luxuriant black thatch.

She slowly undid the hooks and eyes of the whalebone corset, and her body emerged from it with the marks of the stays imprinted on her flesh. Doc eased the loose gown off her shoulders and ran his fingertips inside the long, reddened indentations on her torso. She kicked off her shoes and sat back on the bed. In a few expert moves, she uncovered his cock and balls. She lay on her back on the bed and waited demurely for him to enter her. As his cock slid deep into her moist opening, Doc remembered he was still wearing his hat.

CHAPTER THREE

Raider stood at the bar of a San Francisco tavern, a place that went out of its way to appeal to all that was ornery in mankind. It had once been a fancy gambling parlor, but somewhere along the line the owner had given up fixing the damage inflicted on the furnishings by the customers. The large painting above the bar of a reclining nude redhead had the pussy and nipples shot out of the canvas, plus some stray holes punctured elsewhere by less accurate triggermen. Mirrors and etched-glass panels, shattered in cobweb patterns, hung delicately in their frames. Four girls danced to piano music every so often, lifting their dresses and petticoats in the latest French saucy manner. There were no limits, few rules, and no credit at the gaming tables. A man could take the girls upstairs or somewhere else, as he pleased. He was also expected to settle his own arguments. The management did not bother the customers, and in turn had no wish to be bothered by them.

This was what Raider regarded as true democracy. The quality of the whiskey could have been better, but then again

35

it could have been worse. He was not a man who demanded perfection. And he was enjoying this breather between assignments. The Sierra job, with McPhee along as a beginner, had worked out well. After getting to San Francisco, he had sent a brief assessment of McPhee, as required, to the Chicago office—just a few words saying he would do fine. Raider knew he would be in the Napa Valley by the time some deskbound worrier sent a reply demanding more information.

"What they want all the time is information," Raider said thickly to the miner next to him at the bar. "And what do they do with it when they get it? Nothing. That's what they do with it."

The miner looked warily at Raider. He had no idea what this big hombre was talking about and had no wish to contradict him.

After a while Raider was joined by Willie McPhee and Paul Heron, who dropped out of a poker game when the stakes started to go over their heads.

Paul complained, "All you need is one crazy miner and a professional cardplayer to call him, and the pair of them will take the game out of everyone's reach."

Raider nodded. His Pinkerton's pay never allowed him much in the way of high-stakes games either. Bitter experience had taught Raider he would never strike it rich at a card table.

They talked for a while, never mentioning the work they had to do. They were due to set out next day, and that would be soon enough. Paul and Willie got lured into another low-stakes game while Raider continued to drink steadily at the bar.

"Watch it!" the miner next to Raider yelled in warning.

Raider ducked and stepped fast to his left, turning as he did so to meet face on with whatever was behind him.

The bottle missed the back of his head. Raider's big right hand closed around the arm of the man who had swung it. The little guy's face was at the level of Raider's shirtfront.

"What's your trouble, mister?" Raider ground out.

He wrenched the corked, half-full whiskey bottle from the man's grasp and placed it on the bar behind him. Then he pulled the man's gun from its holster and tossed it over the bar so that it landed on the floor on the other side.

Raider shook him. "What's your trouble?"

The small man, very drunk, looked at Raider in a kind of confused way.

"You ever see me in your life before?" Raider bellowed. "What have you against me?"

When the man didn't answer, Raider pushed him away.

"I'd have clobbered the bastard," the miner said.

Raider laughed. "I don't know what it is, but often someone who maybe lives a quiet and lawful life all year long goes out on the town one night, swallows a gutful of liquor, and picks on what he thinks is the meanest and biggest badman in the place. For some reason, a lot of them decide that's me." He grinned and fingered a couple of scars. "Fast little bastards. Like that one. Come out of the timber at you when you never even knew they were there. A few have got to me. Caught me by surprise."

The miner looked along the bar "He's still staring at you like he wants to kill you."

Raider couldn't care less. He bought the miner a drink and forgot about the whole incident.

"You were lucky to find me still here," Alice whispered to Doc Weatherbee, cuddling her naked body against his and nestling her head on his shoulder. "I got this live-in job, and I move there tomorrow. God knows what would have happened to me if you hadn't given me this hotel room and food money. I don't think I'd have ended up in a respectable job."

"You *have* other talents," Doc said playfully.

She scratched him. "That's what I'm afraid of. You know what I get to learn on this job—real German and French cooking. The woman who hired me is the wife of a gold miner who struck it rich and now has a mansion on Nob Hill. They've come back from Europe, and she wants to live in style—with all sorts of special food. She tested me in the kitchen after I answered her newspaper notice. Next time you're back in San Francisco, maybe I'll know how to make you a real good dish."

"You already know how to do that," Doc said, letting his hands wander over her body.

"That damn Doc Weatherbee," Willie McPhee said as he left the tavern with Paul Heron and Raider. "I never seen a man with such a thing for women. Talk about moths around a flame."

"Crap," Raider said shortly.

"I wouldn't know," Paul said mildly. "I'm a married man. What do I know about women?"

They made their way none too steadily up a steep street toward their hotel.

Raider looked at some piles of lumber. "They'll be banging with hammers on that shit at first light tomorrow. Don't do much to ease a man's headache."

"Headache?" Willie asked.

"You don't have one now," Raider said. "But wait till you wake up this morning with all these goddamn carpenters hammering and sawing additions onto this dumb city, as if it ain't twice too big already. I sometimes can't hardly believe what folks'll do so they can live like bees or ants. Every time I come to San Francisco, they've build more on—with still more piles of lumber waiting to be hammered together."

"I kinda like this place," Willie said, looking about him.

"Just goes to show you're halfway to becoming a bee or an ant," Raider warned.

They were continuing this deep conversation when a group of men stepped out of the shadows and confronted them in the street. There were eleven in all, dressed in shabby patched city clothes, with pale thin city faces, stunted men who had never had enough to eat, the sons of men who had gone hungry. Not one of them would have lasted a day on a ranch, in a mine, or laying rails. They carried two-foot lengths of new cut timber. One had a big bowie knife. They spoke to each other like Raider, Willie, and Paul were incapable of hearing them.

"Watch the big one. He's carrying a gun."

"He can't walk straight. He couldn't hit a house with it."

"He'd shoot hisself in the foot trying to git it out of the holster."

"Hit him."

"Enough—"

"They got money."

Raider motioned for Willie and Paul to stand back while he walked forward to meet the gang, his fists clenched at his sides. Willie and Paul had been about to reach for their revolvers, which they carried concealed when in the city— unlike Raider, who never changed the way he looked or behaved from Fifth Avenue to the Badlands to the blue Pacific. Willie and Paul reckoned they could have scared off the eleven men with a couple of shots in the air, but Raider was having none of that. He lumbered forward, gun hand nowhere near the handle of his Remington .44.

When the eleven men saw Raider stumbling at them with his big fists clenched, they exchanged cunning leers. They sidestepped and maneuvered like a pack of coyotes, running this way and that to seek the advantage. They might as well have been trying to catch a rockslide off balance as catch Raider coming at them.

Raider surged into them, laying about him with his fists. He drove his foot into the face of a man sitting half stunned, scattering his teeth like necklace beads across the street.

When one of them tackled Raider under the knees and tried to bring him to the ground, Raider dropped to a fast kneel on the man's rib cage, setting off a series of crackles like a burning fuse as the ribs fractured and snapped. Two men beat him across the head and shoulders with lengths of timber until he straightened up, grabbed a head in each hand, and brought them together with a loud knock of bone on bone. The others ran away down the street.

Raider stepped out of the pile of half-conscious moaning bodies about him and waved his finger at Willie McPhee. "It don't do for a Pinkerton to go using his gun in the middle of the night in a big-city place like this. You have to be real quiet. Without disturbing the peace."

Willie tried not to laugh, because he saw Raider was serious.

Next morning was clear, and Doc Weatherbee called early at the hotel for the three of them. While Doc's mood was as breezy and sunny as the California morning, Raider, Willie, and Paul were vague and fogbound with hangovers. Raider's belly was troubling him, and he refused the breakfast of prairie cakes and eggs Doc bought for them, settling for a quart of beer instead.

As usual, Doc had everything arranged. "You three take the steamer north up the bay to Vallejo. From there you take the Napa Valley Railroad to Napa City, and farther on if that's what you decide. I reckon Paul has to present himself to the railroad company in Napa City as soon as possible."

"As soon as I step on that train in Vallejo, I start my job," Heron said. "They don't want to see my face in that office. They want me out where none of them care to go. The trouble spot is just north of the town of St. Helena, a ways up the valley. I say all three of us stay on that train and see what kind of trouble we run into."

"We going to be together?" Willie asked a little anxiously.

Raider laughed and slapped him on the shoulder. "No way, boy. I'm going to be depending on you to hold your own."

"Just stay away from Raider," Doc advised. "Being around him is your surest way of getting slaughtered."

"You'll be all right along with me, Willie," Raider said hotly. "Just watch you don't hang your hopes on a dude like him." He pointed scornfully at Doc. "Son of a bitch don't even carry a gun. You'll find him combing his hair instead of backing you up. Or his finger up some pussy instead of on the trigger."

Doc Weatherbee brushed off his derby without bothering to respond to Raider's taunts. Clearly he considered it beneath his dignity to do so.

Raider spat on the floorboards a half inch from one of Doc's brightly polished shoes. The refreshment house owner scuttled across to protest, but changed his mind when he took a close look at Raider, and toweled up the offending saliva with an apology—as if himself had been responsible for it. A minute later a Chinese kitchen hand was sent to place two brass spittoons on the floor, one on either side of Raider's chair.

Raider laughed, his anger at Doc forgotten. "This is what really gets me in the city. Them little insects are watching a man all the time, trying to guess where his foot will fall next."

Doc saw them off on the steamer, which didn't leave the dock for some time after they boarded. To be absolutely sure nothing went wrong, Doc stayed on the wharf till the boat pulled away. Raider, Willie, and Paul stood at the white rail of the upper deck, breathing in sharp marine air that washed out the dust and grime that had stuck in their brains from the night before. Even Raider was looking in a cheerful mood when the steamer tooted as she pulled away from land. The boat had gone only a short distance from shore when it started to pitch and toss. There were no big waves on the bay, only small sharp teeth of water that jagged above the surface for a moment and sank down. Doc found it hard to understand how such little waves could cause a big boat to heave and buck like it did. Apparently the fresh breeze that had blown the fog from the water and clouds from the sky packed more wallop than a landsman would guess. Last thing Doc noticed on the steamer was Raider half doubled over, staring back at him in hate. Willie was heaving up his breakfast over the rail into the sea.

Doc strode leisurely past activities on the docks and new

warehouses being built. One of the chief reasons for Doc's good humor was that he was on his way to see Judith. He hadn't seen her in almost ten days. She would be rearing to go.

She was. Judith beat her front hooves on the stable floor with excitement as she was harnessed up. Doc led the mule to the drinking trough and went into a cavernous carriage house to check on his wagon. It was a small Studebaker, filled with homeopathic medicines, nostrums, health restorers, invigorators, and so forth. But it was not these medicine bottles that Doc was interested in checking. After a quick look around to make sure he was alone, he lifted the floorboards of the wagon to reveal a secret compartment. Rifles, shotguns, two Gatling guns, ammunition, explosives, a telegraph and gravity batteries, a Premo Sr. camera and developing equipment—the amount and variety of items tightly packed into the compartment sometimes amazed even Doc himself, who had done the packing. Everything looked in order. All the narrow strips of fabric placed about the opening to the secret compartment had been undisturbed. Pilferers always contented themselves with the medicine bottles and never thought to look further. The medicines were all harmless, and Doc did not begrudge a few of them to ailing thieves. Acquired in that way, the medicines might even do the thieves good.

Doc had his own theories about medicine. When he first bought the mule and wagonload of medicines from a homeopathic physician in Carson City, he had thought only of the cover this would provide him as a Pinkerton operative in the field. Few people deny a medical doctor access, no matter how doubtful his qualifications. And even the most heavily armed outlaws get worms, break bones, have mysterious internal pains. The medical disguise had worked wonders for Doc over the years. But what he had not foreseen when he had bought the outfit was that innocent people he had no wish to hurt would come to him and demand medical attention, and that in order to maintain his disguise he would have to give it to them.

Which got Doc to thinking fast. First he got rid of all medicines that could cause physical harm to people. Next he vowed never to try to cure someone who was really sick—only those with minor ailments or imaginary ones. He always steered someone who was genuinely ill to a qualified physician—not that that did much good most of the time.

Doc's big medical discovery was made early: that almost any pill or ointment will cure almost any minor or imaginary ailment if the patient believes it will. His was a variation on the old theme of faith healing, and it worked better than Doc would previously have imagined possible. He enjoyed the added benefit of doing good for people as a sideline to his Pinkerton duties.

Doc dusted off the containers of blood purifier, liver regulator, hop bitters, swamp root, Indian cough cure, ocean weed heart remedy, and autumn leaf extract for females. He shook out the banners that hung on either side of his Studebaker wagon: DOCTOR WEATHERBEE—HOMEOPATHIC MEDICINES—FREE CONSULTATION. Then he fetched Judith from the watering trough and hitched her to the wagon. Judith did not balk in the city traffic—in fact it was all Doc could do to stop her from racing horses and mules in the narrow streets. When Judith got a competitive notion, she'd try to outrun anything with four hooves, and if she got left behind, she was inclined to play dirty. Doc was feeling so pleased with himself this fine morning, he forgot about his mule's mean streak, thinking everyone, including mules, must be thinking thoughts as kind as his own.

A high-stepping gray mare between the shafts of a chaise got Judith's dander up. The top of the chaise was folded back, and its occupants, an elegant woman and a self-important-looking man, gave Doc and his wagon a supercilious stare, like he was littering *their* street with *his* presence. Maybe the gray mare tried a similar look on Judith and that was what set her off, but more likely it was simply the self-assured trot of the horse that riled the mule. As the mare passed, pulling the light two-wheeled carriage, Judith lurched forward and savagely jerked the wagon along behind her as she tried to keep abreast of the horse.

It was an uneven contest from the start. There was no way Judith could have kept up with the high-stepping mare even without an ungainly wagon to pull. The mule reached her head sideways and bit viciously at the mare's shoulder. Her long chisel teeth sank into the horse's hide; the mare whinnied in fright and pain, lurched to one side, and broke a shaft of the chaise.

Doc pulled hard on the reins and dragged Judith to a halt.

"You folks all right?" he called back to the two in the chaise.

The woman patted her forehead with a lace handkerchief.

The man sputtered, "Impertinent pup!"

Doc smiled and raised his derby. "If you're not feeling well, I could sell you some medicine."

He flicked the reins. Judith didn't move. Doc soon saw why. She was busy leaving the gray mare a parting message in the middle of the street. . . .

When they got to dockside, the sight of water and boats made Judith less frisky, almost as if she had a premonition of what was to come.

"They told me I could find a schooner that'd take this mule and wagon to Napa City," Doc said to a seafaring man in a blue wool sweater.

"Sure you can. You got six feet of water at least at high tide on the river at Napa. Any of these shallow-draft schooners can go in there. Most do, with freight that's too much trouble moving twice, from the dock to the steamer and from that to the train. Sing out. One of these boats'll be leaving when the tide turns."

The mule looked worried when she saw the wagon rise into the air on cables, swing out over the ship, and be lowered to the deck. When the dockworkers slung a broad canvas band beneath her belly and hoisted her high into the air at the end of a rope, her four legs dangled and her head looked from side to side till she spotted Doc standing on the wharf. Judith gave him an accusing look. Doc felt guilty and had to look away.

The train steamed north from the town of Rutherford, two-thirds of the way up the Napa Valley. Paul Heron sat in the first coach and looked out the window at the passing countryside. He had been noticing how the neatly planted rows of grape vines, growing on wires strung between stakes, had eaten into the cattle-rearing ranchland of the valley floor.

"You see more of that every year," a fellow passenger growled when Heron remarked on the vines. "Spreading like a cancer on good grassland."

Another passenger laughed. "Spoken like a true cattle-man, neighbor. I grow vines. You'll see the day when this whole valley floor will be covered with them. This is one of the few places we know of where the soil and climate are perfect for grapes. You can raise cattle anywhere. Pity to waste the Napa Valley on them."

The cattleman only snorted good-humoredly at his neighbor's ribbing. Out the window, Paul could see tawny hills separating the mountains from the valley floor. Farmhouses were large and looked prosperous. After the parched country of the prairies and high plains, this valley sure looked like a paradise. A man could do worse than settle here. After he cleaned up this mess on the railroad, with the Pinkertons' help, he'd bring his family out. They would like it here. He might even plant a few grapes himself and bottle some homemade wine.

The train started to slow as it came to the next town. The rancher stood and took his Stetson from the overhead rack. The winery man reached for his bag.

"I thought you two said you lived up Calistoga way," Heron said. "This should only be St. Helena. Ain't you leaving the train kind of early?"

"You will too if you got any sense," the rancher said. "Haven't you heard about the trouble on the line?"

"Some," Heron allowed. "It didn't seem to be enough

to chase me off a train though."

The rancher laughed. "Then you're a braver man than me. Or a more foolish one. I don't aim to shoot it out with a bunch of roughnecks. It's a lot easier to get off at St. Helena, like they want you to, and ride the rest of the way home. You'll see every other man on this train do the same thing, 'cept maybe for some newcomers like you who don't know any better."

"Will they stop the train for sure?" Heron asked.

"Who knows what they'll do? Their protest started out with reasonable men who wouldn't harm no one. Now, if they don't string you up or set fire to you for the fun of it, maybe you'll get robbed or stomped. Good luck to you, mister."

"It's not as bad as he makes it out," the winery man added. "They haven't robbed any passengers—though they've made a few get out and walk. Been a lot of killings, but they were railroad security men and land agents and such."

That wasn't much comfort to Paul. When the train began to move forward again, he noted he was the only one left in the coach.

In the coach behind Paul Heron's, Willie McPhee had just been through a similar conversation. Only the conductor was now left with him in that coach.

"How come you stay on in your job?" Willie asked him.

"So far they haven't hurt none of the crews who regularly work the line. Only guards and such. We don't give them no resistance, and I guess they reckon we're just doing our jobs. It's not us who says what goes. We just do what we're told. So there's no blame attached to us."

"Blame for what?"

"Those squatters feel the railroad's in collusion with big land developers, helping to drive them off."

Willie guessed where the conductor's sympathies lay and saw that the man was being careful with what he said to him, not knowing who he was.

Willie said, "Nobody told me anything when I bought my ticket."

"You get your full money back if the train don't get to your ticketed destination. So at least you travel this far for free."

Raider, in the third car back, opened the window as the train slowed and stuck his head out. He had already guessed the train crews had some sort of unspoken agreement with the robbers so they wouldn't get hurt. The railroad men had his sympathy—they had to walk a thin line, with their jobs to lose on one hand and perhaps their lives on the other. Raider could see right now that his first job would be to relieve this pressure, and the best way he knew how to do that was to test the willingness of those putting on the pressure. He pulled his head in only when he saw a group of men by the side of the track ahead. The train, with great belches of smokes and hissing steam, ground to a halt.

Raider opened the door and climbed down to the ground. He saw the conductor jump down from the coach ahead of him and walk to the group of men, who were shouting up at the engineer and fireman in the locomotive. Raider saw Willie McPhee looking at him for a signal from inside the second coach. Raider shook his head slightly and walked on. Paul Heron was deep in a newspaper at a window in the first coach, apparently oblivious to the delay. The conductor was arguing with some of the men. They in turn were beckoning three empty wagons to advance.

"We'll take what we can, and destroy what we can't," one man was telling the conductor in a belligerent tone as Raider came within earshot.

They all stopped talking as he neared. He ignored them and continued to the front of the locomotive. A rail had been lifted from the roadbed and laid just a foot to the side. The spikes and hammers lay beside the rail.

Raider returned and faced the group. "Who did that?"

"I did."

"Me too."

"And me."

"Fix it!" Raider barked at one man.

When this unarmed man stood his ground, Raider caught him by an arm and threw him against the steel spokes of a locomotive wheel. The wheel rim cut his forehead, and he sank dazed on the wooden sleepers.

Raider had already turned to the next man. He too was unarmed. Raider pushed him and then booted him in the ass.

"Go fix that rail!" he yelled and slung another man after him.

The two men did not dare refuse. They stood at one end of the rail and waited for others to help.

Raider got what he was waiting for. As he stepped toward the group, most of the men backed off a few paces. There were more than a dozen there—some armed with iron bars, shotguns, or pistols—but most were not fighting men. They backed off, even though they were only up against one man. They had seen his ferocious strength, and now they saw his right hand hover over the handle of the big revolver on his right hip. The message was deadly clear. They all retreated, except for one, who stood his ground squarely.

"That's my brother," this man said, nodding toward one of the men. "Better keep your hands off him."

"Be pleased to oblige," Raider said and kicked the brother in the gut, hardly taking his eyes off the man facing him down. When he got no reaction, Raider kicked the staggering man again and again, booting him until the man broke and ran almost all the way to the rail.

"I want that rail laid back where it was so the train can take me where it's supposed to," Raider said calmly. "You won't find no percentage in messing with me. That's just some friendly advice. Tell your buddies to lay that rail in place."

Raider had noticed how two other men had come to stand along with his opponent. All three were ready to draw their revolvers.

"You win," the man said to Raider. "Fellas, put that rail back. Forget this train."

Hoping his words had lulled Raider, he made a surprise move for his gun. Slow to believe any man's words, Raider's response was fast. The long barrel of his Remington .44 cleared the holster leather and his right thumb was cocking the hammer while the other man still fumbled with his weapon. Raider squeezed the trigger and saw a red hole the size of nickel appear on his opponent's dirty white undershirt.

Raider thumbed back the hammer for a second shot, and his eyes traveled fast over the other men. As the man before him crumpled to the ground, the one to the left had almost cleared his weapon from its holster. He paid for being slow in coming to his friend's aid. The Remington spat flame and a .44 slug burrowed its way into his vital parts. He collapsed in a moaning heap beside the first man Raider had shot.

Raider's voice was warm and companionable. "Any man still wearing a gunbelt or holding a gun ten seconds from now had better have already used it."

They outnumbered him and they knew it. They stared back at Raider without moving.

Raider replaced his Remington in its holster without reloading it. He had four cartridges left in the chambers.

"Ten seconds," he repeated.

They still did nothing except stare back. A tall young man had assumed their leadership by standing out before them and calling Raider's bluff.

Then the ten seconds were up. Every man there saw the blur of Raider's gun hand and saw the big pistol kick and roar. The tall young man bit the dust, clutching his left thigh.

There was a moment of absolute silence except for steam hissing from the locomotive and the gasps of the injured man. Then there was a clatter as they all dropped their weapons and gunbelts to the ground. They didn't need to be directed toward the rail. It took half of them only a few minutes to replace the length of steel and drive the spikes to hold it in place. Meanwhile the others loaded the injured man and the two corpses onto one of the wagons they originally had hoped to load with booty.

The conductor waited respectfully for Raider to walk easily back to the coach he had been riding in, climb aboard, and settle in a seat before he signaled to the engineer. Then he jumped aboard himself and the train steamed on to Calistoga.

CHAPTER FOUR

Doc Weatherbee trundled along the valley floor on his wagon. At the top of the thirty-five-mile-long valley he could see Mount St. Helena, a sleeping volcano. He had heard that lava erupting from this mountain swept down the valley and became converted with time into rich soil. The mountain rose into a cone with its top cut off, or more likely blown off. It stood to the north, brooding over the valley, like a formidable stone fortress. Doc hoped the volcano wasn't going to wake again anytime soon.

He followed the Silverado Trail, between the two parallel mountain chains that made the valley, the Napa range on the east and the Mount Hood range on the west. The mountains pushed into the valley, so that at some places it was barely a mile wide while at others it was five miles across. The sides of the ranges were broken by deep canyons, and Doc guessed some of these led off into hidden miniature valleys. As he looked high on the mountains, the green of trees gave way to the purple of chaparral. The most plentiful tree was the Douglas fir, which not only crowned the low conical hills bounding the flat valley floor, but was common in the canyons and on hill slopes, particularly on north and east exposures. Doc noticed also yellow pine, three or four kinds of oak, digger pine, Oregon maple, madrona, and occasional redwoods. Where not cleared for grassland, vine-yards, or orchards, the valley floor was covered thickly by shrubs—manzanita, Parry lilac, buck brush.

Doc regarded the valley as a perfect mixture of wildness and domesticity. Business in cures wasn't great, because folks here were prosperous and each of the small towns had its own legitimate physician. This was even an advantage for Doc, because his time was not taken up in making sales. Yet he got to talk with people and heard the local news. Doc had perfected his approach. First he got people to tell him about their ailments, and they were usually willing to discuss those even when they had no intention of buying medicine. Then, in easy stages, he steered them away from accounts of their sufferings to local gossip.

The big news locally was how a gunfighter had shot up a group of squatters who had stopped the train. Even before Doc heard a description of this desperado, he had a shrewd notion of who he was. Doc learned that the man injured in the incident was a son of Enrico Crevetti, owner of a big winery not far down the trail. It seemed to Doc that if a physician just happened by, they might find some use for him.

He turned into a heavily rutted trail that ran between two big areas of vines. The winery was a large building con-structed of gray stone. A big frame house stood several hundred yards beyond it. Field-workers were harvesting grapes in one part of the vineyard. They filled baskets with bunches of fruit and tipped the full baskets into a waiting horse-drawn cart. The vines nearest Doc had already been picked clean. The high-sided carts loaded with grapes were lining up at the winery. Men and women rushed about. Many spoke in Italian. They were in the middle of the harvest. Nobody had time to feel sick or buy medicine.

"Come back next month, Doctor. We'll all need you

then," one man called to him and drew laughter from others.

"You gotta have time if you want to be sick," another tried.

"It's a luxury."

"Only the rich can be sick. Me gotta work."

"Can you cure yourself, Doctor?"

Doc Weatherbee was used to this kind of good-natured ribbing. If they weren't so genuinely busy, they would start to come to him in due course to describe their physical woes. A short, squat old man dressed in European style wandered out of the big stone winery and waved his stick to Doc in greeting.

"Bad time for you to come, Doctor," he said with a strong Italian accent. "All us Crevettis are harvesting the grapes— even my grandchildren." He pointed his cane off among the vines, where sure enough Doc could see children's heads bobbing among the green leaves. "My children, their children, nephews, nieces, people from the old country, anyone who needs a job, you yourself if you want—everyone's welcome to lend a hand this time of year at the Crevetti winery."

Doc smiled. "No thanks, my schedule won't allow for that. Are you Enrico Crevetti?"

The old man was clearly flattered that a stranger would know his name. "That's who I am."

"I had some of your zinfandel in San Francisco," Doc said. "I liked it so much I tried your riesling. Several bottles in fact."

"When you see the name Enrico Crevetti on a wine label, Doctor, you can depend on it. What about my Rhenish muscatel? Haven't you tried that?"

"I haven't seen any, but I will first chance I get."

"No time like the present. I'm only in the way here— that's what happens when you get old. You show all the young people how to do things and before you know what's happening, they've learned how to do it better than you ever could and now you're only holding up everybody and delaying things with your old-fashioned ways. They'll be relieved to be rid of me for an hour. And I don't suppose they'll get into too much trouble while I'm gone." He hauled himself up alongside Doc on the wagon and pointed with his stick to the frame house. "I'm not going to buy any of your elixirs and such. I want you to change the dressing and look at a gunshot wound one of my sons has. I reckon I can settle the bill with riesling or muscatel, eh?"

"Fair enough," Doc agreed and urged Judith on.

"Only you must take care of that wound first. I don't want you touching my son with less than a clear head."

Doc looked at the entrance and exit wounds in the muscle of the young man's left thigh.

"No sign of infection," he said. "The doctor in Calistoga did a clean job. Another inch and that bullet would have shattered the bone. You're a lucky man, Mr. Crevetti."

The young man nodded. "Call me Tom. The only Mr. Crevetti around here is my father, and everyone calls him Enrico."

"I heard you tried to shoot it out with a badman down by the tracks?"

"Naw. There was no shoot-out 'tween him and me. He just shot me 'cause I didn't do what he said. He could have killed me if he pleased. I was plain dumb to stand up to him."

His father, coming into the room with bottles and glasses, overheard his son's remarks. "To make a mistake once is something we all do. To make the same mistake twice is dumb. If you get shot again, Tom, then you are stupid. Not now."

Doc finished rebandaging the wound while Enrico opened the wine.

Doc tasted it. "Glad I came."

They drank to Tom's health, and Enrico refilled the glasses.

"You're going to be up and about in a day or two," Doc said to Tom. "Will you be going after the gunfighter who shot you?"

"No, he won't!" old Enrico bawled. "He's needed at the harvest here."

"Pa, there won't be a harvest next year unless we do something about the land grabbers," Tom said.

"You let others take care of it from now on," his father responded. "You've done your bit."

"I don't want to offend you," Doc said, "but I'll say I'm kind of surprised to find a member of this family teaming up with a gang of roughnecks to hold up trains."

In spite of his wounded leg, Tom almost sprang off the couch he was lying on to get at Doc. His father restrained him, but Doc could see that his words had enraged the old man too.

"Do you know anything about what's been happening here, Doctor?" Enrico asked in a cold voice.

"Nothing," Doc said casually. "That's why I asked. I haven't even traveled on the Napa Valley Railroad. I came as far as Napa City by schooner and north to here along the Silverado Trail in my wagon. Is there something I don't understand?"

The two Crevettis stared at him wordlessly, but they were calming down.

"Let me tell you what I've heard," Doc went on, venturing where angels fear to tread. "A group of squatters trying to avoid eviction are extorting money from the railroad to help raise money to buy the land. They've killed nearly a score of people, and law-abiding citizens living in the valley have been terrorized into silence by moonlight riders burning and pillaging."

"You heard all this in San Francisco," Enrico said. It was a statement, not a question.

"Yes," Doc agreed. "When I speak to people in the valley, they don't like to talk about it."

"Certainly they don't," Enrico said with feeling. "They don't want their houses burned over their heads or their crops or stock destroyed on their land. There are moonlight riders who scare people into keeping quiet, but they are not sent out by the squatters. Those trying to drive off the squatters are the ones doing the killing and burning."

"There are two sides to every story," Doc observed. "I seem to have heard only one side."

"Then you listen close to us and you'll hear the other," Tom said.

Enrico held up a hand. "It's your mother calling. The meal is ready. No more talk of this till our food is well digested. Tell him, Doctor. A man can harm his stomach by talking about upsetting things on an empty stomach."

"I'll go along with that," Doc said with a smile.

With Doc's support Tom limped to the big kitchen, and Doc was impressed to see a long table almost sagging under the weight of food. Many of the dishes were Mediterranean, decorated with olives and pimentos. Doc was introduced to many relatives and friends who had come to help with the harvest. There were three very pretty girls, but Doc was effectively removed from conversation with them by polite, heavily muscled males who insisted on leading him away to meet buxom matrons more advanced in years. These ladies were avid for free medical advice and insisted on describing their symptoms to him in detail, with the result that Doc drank a lot and ate a lot and, after the meal, gave away a lot of free samples from his wagon. Anything to get rid of them. He noticed one of the three beauties glancing at him often, and she even laughed openly one time when four very intense, quite large women competed for his attention with the complexities of their illnesses. Later Doc managed to speak to her only long enough to learn that her name was Vittoria.

Brandy warmed the talk between the old man, his son, and Doc Weatherbee.

"Back when the Mexicans owned California," Enrico said, "this valley was divided into nine ranchos. Napa was the name of one of them, called after the river. Tulucay and Caymus were others. Some of the ranchos had been granted to individuals who had provided the Mexican government with money and supplies, as well as in recognition for official services. When California changed hands, the rights of those who had bought or been granted lands under the Mexicans was recognized by the Americans. The Treaty of Guadelupe Hidalgo insured that the United States government had to confirm these rancho titles if they were found valid, and most were. But in many cases the exact extent of a rancho was vague. Some of the surveys had been done by horsemen galloping from point to point and indicating these as the boundary lines. There was hell to pay over that kind of thing, but the biggest trouble was over ranchos that had been claimed on false or at least doubtful titles. The land this house stands on was part of the Paloma rancho. No one knows for sure what happened here except that the original title holder, the Mexican who received the land grant in the first place, sold it to some other Mexicans before California became American. I don't know what happened then, and neither does anyone else. The land became ownerless, and squatters moved in. I was one of them, here in America only two years from Tuscany. I knew maybe a hundred English words, none of them the ones I ever needed. We squatters worked the land, the government put the land in public domain, it became ours. That should have been the end of everything. You think it was?"

"No," Doc said dutifully.

Enrico poured more brandy for the three of them. "You're right, Doctor. Not the end. The beginning. Of trouble. Trouble and more trouble. Till you see my son before you with a bullet hole in his leg."

Doc felt unable to explain his indirect link, through Raider, to Tom's injury. He needed to hear more. "What does stopping trains have to do with all this?"

"Hold your horses there, Doctor," Enrico said. "Hear me out. After we moved here, the Paloma rancho became known as the Prospect ranch. I'd have preferred to call it the Toscana or Arrezzo, something like that, but Prospect it was and I don't recall why. Then a pair of real estate sharks from back east turned up in San Francisco with what they claimed was the original title to this rancho. They went to court. We went to court. That went on for years, even though they lost every time. Finally their title was shown to be a fake. A counterfeit. Nobody accused these real estate sharks, two brothers by the name of Jones, of committing fraud. It was assumed they were victims, not perpetrators. Anyway that was final. Their title wasn't genuine. They had no claim to the land. That sound final to you?"

"Sounds final to me," Doc agreed.

Enrico poured more brandy. "But you're talking about justice—the Jones brothers were talking about land. They aimed to get this ranch by fairs means or foul. Listen to this. They bribed politicians to push a so-called relief act through Congress, a special preemption act that allowed them to take the land from under us by paying us $1.25 an acre. Land bought by George Yount in 1849 for $1.50 an acre is now fetching $125 an acre!"

His son put in, "There's round about five thousand acres here on the Prospect ranch. If the Joneses can force us and the other squatters off the ranch for a total of $6,250, they can sell it off in lots at $125 an acre and make $625,000."

"Buy an acre for $1.25 and sell it for $125, now that's some profit," Doc said. "I see where they'd have lots of cash to make payoffs."

"Before they can sell, they first got to get us off the land," Tom said fiercely.

Doc brought up his chief concern. "How's the railroad involved?"

"The Napa Valley Railroad was built about ten years ago with local funds," Enrico explained. "It's a nice little rail-road, and it has served the community well. This was where the Jones brothers got sneaky clever. They were too smart to try to seize the land the railroad uses over the Prospect ranch. They saw that the railroad lawyers would be a big help to us squatters if our interests coincided, so the Joneses struck a different deal with the railroad company. So long as the company stayed out of the fight, they would receive a free grant for a tract one acre wide the length of their roadbed through the Prospect ranch. The company has agreed to sign the deal and stab us in the back. Once the Jones brothers can point to a legitimate settlement with a railroad, it will considerably weaken the squatters' case against the government. We've been warned about that. And the railroad company people know that. We used to be in this fight together, they and us. But now they've gotten greedy and don't give a damn about us anymore."

Doc took this in and thought about it for a while. Had Raider gunned down innocent men? "What bothers me is hearing about all the men you squatters have been killing on the railroad. Those men weren't responsible."

Enrico muttered in Italian and glowered at his son. He turned to Doc. "I called him names. My son here, a Crevetti, goes around with low-life ruffians. Such things have been part of the trouble here. The confrontation has attracted violent men. They come not to protest but to rob and kill. Those men who were slain when my son was there came to steal furniture that was on that train. They knew Tom and the others would stop the train—"

Tom interrupted. "You have to realize that not every squatter on the Prospect ranch is an angel with a halo. We got some mighty rough people who live in these parts. They're quiet most of the time, but when folks cross 'em, watch out. When we're down there stopping the train—it goes by only four times a day, twice down and twice up—we can't shoo the bad ones off when they decide to join in too. Most of the killings was done by men who don't even live on the Prospect ranch."

"Tell him the truth," his father said.

"All right," Tom conceded. "I told half the truth. So we hired guns to come in because the railroad set their goons on us. Our boys are tougher than theirs—one hell of a lot tougher. Things got out of control sometimes and people got shot. Now the railroad has itself another gunslinger riding the train. Fella by the name of Raider. He's the one who shot me. He's been kicking ass to make sure all the trains go through, and now people have started to ride all the way to Calistoga again. If we stand up against this gunslinger, we'll get blasted away. So what can we do except hire guns to take him?"

Doc did not like the way things were turning out.

Napa City, at the southern end of the valley, was a pretty town, proud of its new stone bridges across the Napa River, some completed and others still being built. The town had first been settled in 1847 and now boasted two banks, two newspapers, and two tanneries. Less than fifty miles north of San Francisco, Napa City was connected to it three times a week by steamer up the river. Twice a day the trains passed down to Vallejo, where steamer service to San Francisco was much more frequent, and twice a day the train passed up the valley through Napa City, Yountville, Oakville, and St. Helena to the end of the line at Calistoga. Most valley residents could make the round trip to San Francisco in twelve hours.

Raider and Paul Heron stayed at the San Pablo Hotel, once the residence of a hidalgo, with tiles and a courtyard reminiscent of warmer climes farther south. Neither of them got too popular in the town. They rode the trains each day, and word was soon out that Heron was the railroad's new security man and that Raider had killed two squatters. Since that had happened there had been some vandalism and obstructions on the line, but no one had stuck around to try robbing the train or harassing its passengers. People were riding all the way to Calistoga again.

Willie McPhee had been left at Calistoga, and like Doc Weatherbee he had not so far been connected by others with Raider and Paul. They wanted to keep it that way.

Raider was none too bothered by the fact that people avoided him. Respectable townspeople normally did anyway. Paul was more upset and questioned anyone who allowed him to do so. Raider ignored Paul's doubts, telling him they could rely on Doc to find out the real truth of things for them. Thus when they saw Doc get on the morning train at St. Helena for the run down the valley, they looked forward to some hard information. Paul told Doc their meeting place in a few words, and all three left the train in Napa City and made their way separately to the San Pablo Hotel. Paul was waiting in Room 16 when Doc got there.

Raider arrived after Doc. He looked about the room. "Nothing to drink?"

"No," Paul said. "This is serious and—"

"Hell, if it's serious, all the more reason to have a drink," Raider insisted.

"I'm hungry, too," Doc added.

Paul sighed. "I'll send Won Gee to get something."

He went out the door and called down the staircase. When he came back in the room, Doc gave them a quick account of what he had learned so far, stressing the fact that the squatters were perhaps in the right—or at least that the railroad they were working for might not be wholly in the right.

"I'm not sure how all this fits in with the code," Doc said, knowing he didn't have to explain the Pinkerton code to Paul Heron. "I've telegraphed a report to Chicago, and I'll pass on instructions."

"Mr. Pinkerton warned me against this small railroad," Paul mused.

"He'd warn God against heaven," Raider said, "except the man is a damn heathen." He turned belligerently on Doc. "You trying to make out I shot harmless squatters up there on the tracks?"

"No. There's been a bad element hanging about to see what they can steal off the trains. It seems they've been doing some of the killing along with those hired guns. Some weren't even residents on the ranch."

Raider spat on the carpet. "Sounds like bullshit to me. Ones I seen hardly ain't worth the powder and lead to get rid of. Be cheaper to twist grass ropes and hang 'em."

"They're not all bad, Raider," Doc said.

"You been sleepin' with their sisters, that how you know?" Raider asked with an edge in his voice.

"I've been talking with families," Doc said. "Sure, you got to defend yourself against a few crazy ones and scheming outsiders, but I tell you most of these people are decent."

Raider's eyes blazed. "If you could keep your goddamn slippery hands off their women's butts and come down to the rails and hold onto a gun handle for a change, maybe your opinions will change and we'll get the job done."

"It's not that simple, Raider," Doc said. "I wish it was. Trouble is, we may be protecting the wrong people."

"I'm protecting trains, not people," Raider shouted.

Paul Heron kept his mouth shut and his eyes out the window. He remembered hearing that Doc had once lost a tooth in a difference of opinion with Raider. Which wasn't a lot, Paul supposed, if one took Raider's size and ferocity into account.

Won Gee arrived with whiskey and pork chops. A Chinese girl followed with plates, utensils, and vegetables. Paul thanked and paid them, and Won Gee left the room. The girl stayed.

"You too," Paul said. "Go."

She shook her head and stayed put.

Paul called after Won Gee, "Hey, you forgot someone."

"She stay," the young Chinese man told him. "She serve you drinks, food."

"And perhaps listen to what we say," Paul added.

"She not understand much English," Won Gee said. "Bad Chinese people cause trouble. She safe here."

"Let her stay," Doc said. "After we eat, we can take a walk outside and I'll put some plans to you."

They did this. On Main Street between First and Second they found themselves between two groups of Chinese men. Most carried meat cleavers. A few had revolvers. Whites caught on the block between the two opposing Oriental groups ran through any house doors that were still open, and the doors were shutting fast. Raider and Doc were not in the habit of running. Raider's hand hovered above his Remington .44, but he made a point of not drawing the weapon. Doc as usual was unarmed—and unconcerned. Paul stood rooted to the spot, eyes wide with fear, standing in the street between the two Asian gangs closing in on each other.

"Let's walk through before the fight starts," Raider said.

Doc nodded.

The three began to thread their way through one of the advancing groups. The set faces and unwavering eyes of the Chinese men, blades glittering in their hands, ignored them. They might as well not have existed as the Chinese gang swept around and past them.

This was too much for Paul Heron. He panicked. He headed for a half-open window in a private house and dived headfirst inside. Almost. Because his bulky girth caught in the window frame and left his backside and legs still outside.

The two Chinese gangs made contact. They hacked at each other with the cleavers and fired some wild pistol shots. Doc and Raider gave up trying to push Paul all the way in through the window or pull him out again. He was firmly stuck, with his big ass wedged in the frame and his short legs kicking wildly. Only a few feet away, the Chinese waved the broad blades of their cleavers at one another and shouted loudly. Doc and Raider guarded the exposed posterior of their friend.

They saw one man get his cheek sliced neatly open by a razor-sharp cleaver. Others got deep cuts on their heads and arms, but the whole affair seemed more a show of force than a fight to the death. Doc knew the Chinese often referred to whites as ghosts, but this was surely the first time he had ever felt like one—he and Raider ignored in the middle of a fight.

CHAPTER FIVE

Willie McPhee sat in the Pair of Fives saloon in Calistoga. This was the main trouble spot in town, and Willie had been frequenting the place every day. To his surprise, no one had hassled him. He didn't gamble, didn't mouth off on various subjects, took it very easy with booze. If anyone asked, he was looking for work. What kind? Made no matter. When a man carries a gun and is in no particular hurry, a lot of people don't have to question the kind of work he does. Especially since Willie was real young. Most of the hired guns were little more than kids. The ones who lived long enough to grow older got sense and tried some other less risky line of work.

Willie looked typical in that he was young, jumpy, and fast-moving. No one ever knew how quick one of these kids was going to be if they were pushed. And anyone who hung out in the Pair of Fives had to have a mean streak in him somewhere.

Some of those causing trouble down on the railroad liked to drink at the Pair of Fives. They boasted at the bar of stopping and robbing the trains—always keeping vague about exactly when and which one. Willie figured some of it for bar talk. Though he couldn't always tell for sure.

The saloon was not much to look at—certainly no gambling palace or fancy house. The dark walls and sparse gaslights made the place dim, which was all right with most of the customers, who had no wish to be illumined in bright clear light.

When Raider walked in, he caused a silence. Some knew him by sight, and others by repute. No one spoke to him, not even to cuss him. He came to the bar alongside Willie and ordered a whiskey. The barkeep was a bit slow.

"Gimme a drink, fool!" Raider yelled.

"Keep it down, fella," Willie told him. "I like peace and quiet."

"You talkin' to me?" Raider asked, looking as if he knew some kind of mistake must have happened and he was giving the man a chance to right his mistake.

"I said to keep it down," Willie growled. "You make too much noise."

Raider only laughed, crashed his hand down on top of the bar, and yelled at the barkeep again for some whiskey. Plainly the big gunfighter with the black mustache wasn't taking the much smaller man next to him very seriously. The others in the saloon had a kind of morbid curiosity to find out how far Willie might go. They backed off a ways and stood around so they would miss nothing, yet not get hit with stray bullets. There wasn't that much happening in Calistoga that anyone could afford to skip entertainment like this. Free, too.

"Don't serve this hombre no drink, John," Willie ordered.

The barkeep froze. He had been just about to pour a whiskey for Raider and place the bottle beside his glass. There was an unmistakable threat in Willie's voice. And there was no mistaking the look in Raider's eye—that man was going to cause big trouble if he didn't get his drink. The barkeep was caught between a rock and a hard place.

He did the only thing he could do—hesitated, and kept on hesitating without doing one thing or the other, waiting till the two badmen on the other side of the bar solved the problem between themselves.

Raider gazed down at the smaller man next to him. He seemed perplexed, even shocked, for a moment. Then his face twisted into a scowl of rage.

"You little son of a bitch. I'm gonna drill you full of holes."

And he went for his gun.

Willie McPhee outdrew him. Raider found himself looking into the eye of Willie's .45.

"Well, what you waiting for?" Raider ground out, letting his own gun sink back into its holster. "You know how to pull the trigger, don't you?"

Willie looked along the barrel at him. "You're getting to be an old man, hombre. Your hands don't move fast as they once did. Neither does your brain. I ain't going to kill you 'cause of that. Now go drink somewhere else."

Raider did a slow turn, then turned and stalked out of the saloon with as much dignity as he could muster.

Willie McPhee was back in his Calistoga hotel room no more than a couple of hours when word had spread all over the upper valley how the jumpy little dude in the Pair of Fives had faced down the railroad's deadly hired gun named Raider. A lot of folks found it hard to believe, claimed it was the whiskey talking, until they heard the same story from several witnesses. A crowd of people had seen it happen.

"Why in hell didn't McPhee shoot him?" more than one man asked in the Pair of Fives later that night.

"He had the chance," a hook-nosed man named Carver said. "Some of us wouldn't have missed out on that opportunity."

"You're talkin' God's honest truth, Carver," another man said. "T'would be doin' a civic duty."

"Yeah, Cale, you're civic-minded all right." Carver

laughed. "You think this McPhee kid is looking for work?"

"I think so," John the barkeep put in. "But my guess is he's mighty particular and in no sort of hurry."

"Mark of a successful man," Carver observed. "Where you say he's staying, John?"

Carver and Cale had no trouble persuading McPhee to leave his hotel room and ride out to the edge of town with them in the dark.

"He sure as hell don't look like no gunfighter to me," Cale said under his breath to Carver as they rode along.

"That's 'cause he's crazy," Carver said in a low voice. "Crazy men make the best gun-toters. See the way he just upped and rode out with us into the night without hardly a word? He don't give a fuck about us. No more scared of us than he would be of two jackrabbits."

"Hush down, he'll hear you," Cale warned. "I agree he's a mighty peculiar individual. But what I meant was he don't seem to have a fightin' streak in him."

Carver snickered. "So why don't you try him, Cale?"

"I'm thinking of a way in which maybe I will."

Cale would say nothing more, and soon the three horsemen reached the edge of the town of Calistoga and could no longer rely on the lights from house windows to show them the way.

"Just a bit farther," Carver shouted to Willie, "and you'll be able to see the lights of an old ranch house. I think it was built before this town was, which accounts for it being so close."

In a short time they saw lanterns hanging in trees, and in their light Willie could make out an old Spanish-style house. When he got nearer, he saw it was in poor shape—even falling down in places. Willie wondered whether he should feel scared. He was so far out of his depth in what he was doing now, he didn't even know whether he should be scared or not. So he wasn't.

As he rode slowly through the darkness, Willie recalled how Doc Weatherbee had arrived in Calistoga that morning by train and sent around a Chinese girl to the hotel to fetch him. Willie never got the full story, but it seemed to him that the girl and a Chinese boy who was waiting with Doc, both born in China in different provinces, had fallen in love and caused a riot between their two factions on a street in Napa City. Back in China the warlords of their provinces were traditional enemies, and it took only a spark to set the bad feelings ablaze again on this side of the Pacific. Doc helped them leave Napa City aboard the train, and now they were heading north on foot to Idaho. They had saved money and wanted to farm, but were prohibited, as Chinese, from owning land in the United States. The boy said he was from Kuangtung province and had relatives who farmed terraces on the southern exposures of remote slopes in the forests near McCall, Idaho. He said the Chinese up there grew all kinds of vegetables, had big plantings of rhubarb and strawberries, had apples trees and even vineyards.

"You asking me to help a Chinaman and a Chinagirl do something illegal?" Willie asked Doc.

"No one's asking you to help them on the farm," Doc told him. "I helped them out of Napa City because their lives were threatened. If they commit a crime in Idaho by growing strawberries, that's not my affair. I'm helping them to the top of this valley and saying goodbye to them there. You can wait back here for me if you like."

"I'll string along," Willie said sulkily.

Willie had known of Doc's reputation of doing things by the book and was surprised to find him involved in something like this. He guessed that Doc must be feeling he should be setting a better example than this for a Pinkerton beginner. Then Willie decided that Doc couldn't show him any better example than a bit of human kindness.

After the Chinese couple had departed for the Idaho rhubarb slopes, Doc outlines his plan for Willie's and Raider's showdown, with Willie coming out the victor.

"I could never make it look real, Doc," Willie protested.

Willie had been right. Even though Raider had given him

lots of time after calling him a son of a bitch—Doc told him he was to draw on the word "bitch"—even though Raider went on to say something else before going for his own gun, Willie only barely beat him to the draw. And then nearly squeezed the trigger out of a nervous reaction! He hoped Raider hadn't noticed that.

Now these two, Cale and Carver, were going to hire him as a gun so they could rob the train again. Everything Doc said would happen was happening. So far. When Willie had asked Doc what he should do after being hired as a gun, Doc had told him to play it by ear. That was something Willie didn't like the sound of. It meant Doc had no idea what was going to happen next.

About fifteen men were standing about a bonfire in the courtyard of the old Spanish-style ranch house, drinking red wine. There were no introductions and no delays.

"We pay you a share of everything we get from the trains," Carver said to Willie. "One man, one share."

"What do I do?" Willie asked.

"Ride shotgun with us."

"You mean take on any gunfighter who might be on that train?"

"Raider."

"Three shares," Willie countered.

There was some muttering among the men at this but no serious dissent.

Carver waited for the voices to die down. "Three shares. You'll get what you ask."

Then Cale came in from somewhere outside. He brought a broad-shouldered man with him, gave him a pull on a brandy bottle, and pointed to Willie McPhee. Willie took one look at the man's face and guessed Cale had been saying inflammatory things to him. Willie went for his gun.

This time Willie went with his reflexes. He thumbled back the hammer and squeezed the trigger. The poor bastard with Cale saw nothing except this harmless-looking skinny young man till it was too late for him to duck and haul out his Colt.

Willie put a bullet through his open mouth that shattered the neck vertebrae of his spine and caused his head to sag on his left shoulder like a broken doll's.

The man hit the ground and began leaking blood.

Willie blew smoke from the barrel of his gun and re-holstered it. He wondered vaguely if he had kept within the gunfighters' code or had drawn without giving the man an even chance. He began to suspect the latter when he heard Cale saying to Carver, "He got a mean streak in him all right."

"He'll do fine by us," Carver replied. "And it was high time we got rid of that scalliwag you brought in. He was robbing us blind."

There were no more challenges that night to Willie McPhee.

As arranged, Willie met Doc Weatherbee on horseback alongside the rails about halfway between Calistoga and St. Helena. Like San Francisco to the south, the valley had its morning misty fog, and the two men might have collided had not their horses neighed in warning or greeting. Willie briefed Doc rapidly and waited for instructions. He needed some fast because Carver had told him to be ready for the evening train. A second face-off with Raider would be hard to fake.

"You're doing all right, Willie," Doc said when he had finished his account. "You scared?"

"A bit."

"Good," Doc said. "That way you stay careful and keep alive." He unloaded a telegraph key, sets of wires, and a battery from his saddlebags. At the base of a telegraph pole, he looked sadly up at the wires. "Willie, it would tear my suit to hell to have to shinny up this pole."

"Sure, Doc, I'll do it," Willie said eagerly and took the wire leads.

There were certainly some benefits in having Willie around instead of Raider, Doc mused. Except in the case of bad trouble, where he knew he could always depend on the grouchy, disagreeable Raider, and did not know what to expect from this untried novice. How far out on a limb would Willie go to protect a partner? You couldn't ask a man a question like that, since he couldn't truthfully answer it without experiencing it.

Doc tapped out the first message to Raider in Napa City, telling him to expect a package late in the day. Raider would understand the code. His second message, to Chicago, was more straightforward. Although incidents had been halted on the railroad, one or more new ones were about to occur. It was essential that headquarters clear up its relationship with its client—by which Doc meant that Allan Pinkerton should take a close look at whether his men should be involved in this case. Doc had received no answer yet to more direct questions on this matter, and this was by way of a polite reminder.

"I'm finished," Doc called up to Willie, who was clinging to the top of the telegraph pole.

Willie disconnected to leads from the telegraph wires and worked his way down the pole. On the ground, he looked at his hands. "I got some splinters in my palms." He looked at his legs. "And I've ripped my pants."

Doc unconcernedly put the wires and equipment back in his saddlebags, careful not to let them soil his clothes.

After Willie McPhee left for Calistoga, Doc rode his horse for a while toward St. Helena and then cut away from the railroad toward the Crevetti winery. When he came in sight of the large gray stone building, he saw the usual workers hurrying about. Old Enrico Crevetti seemed glad to see him.

Enrico had his usual complaint. "They have no use for me now that I can no longer lift heavy weights and heft casks. I'm only in everybody's way."

Doc had seen for himself that everyone in the family treated the old man courteously. He guessed that Enrico's feeling of uselessness was more in his own mind than in reality—that in his younger days he might have been one of those men who had to control everything personally and found it almost an insult now to see others equally able to perform the tasks he had once reserved for himself.

"You're a newcomer here, Doc," Enrico said. "All you see is this little old white-haired man who rattles on and on. I wasn't always like this. But people don't recall that—they don't even remember me like I was. I just ain't the man I used to be. Only one thing hasn't run down on me. My mouth."

"How's Tom's leg?"

"See for yourself. He's around the place somewhere. Moving slowly, but he's getting about."

"And how's the harvest coming?"

"Very good, though it's late this year," Enrico said. "The grapes are coming in with a high sugar content. I have forty thousand fruit-bearing vines on fifty-five acres. A third of them are Mission grapes, which is the kind the Franciscan fathers originally brought to Mexico from Spain. The Mission grape came to these parts when a mission was founded in 1823 over in Sonoma, just west of those hills. When I first started, I had all Mission grapes. Then I added Muscat, Rose of Peru, Sweetwater, Fountainebleau, Zinfandel....Now I have Johannesberg and Franken Rieslings, Burger, Chasselas, Malaga, Black Malvoisie, Flame Tokay....People laugh at me 'cause I grow them all. Too many varieties, they say. Maybe they're right. Maybe not."

"I noticed a big winery about a mile and a half north of St. Helena," Doc said.

"Biggest this part of the valley. Owned by a native of Mainz, on the Rhine, name of Charles Krug. He has sixty thousand vines on about seventy acres, plus another seven hundred acres of land in grass and orchards. His spread is not part of the Prospect ranch, lucky for him. Krug is a friend of mind. He was one of the first to make wine in the Napa. In 1860 he made five thousand gallons for Colonel Yount at Yountville. Know how many gallons of wine they reckon was made in the valley last year alone?"

"I don't know," Doc said.

"Well, there's supposed to be 2,300,000 fruit-bearing vines that gave more than 700,000 gallons of wine and 12,000 of brandy."

Doc whistled in appreciation at these numbers.

"You get $20 to $40 a ton for grapes," Enrico went on, unstoppable, "and wines fetch twenty to forty cents a gallon wholesale. That's why the land here has gotten so expensive."

"Can't they grow grapes in other places?"

Enrico gestured about him. "Napa Valley is the best place in America. Sure, they grow them to the west of us in Sonoma and to the east of us in the Vaca Valley in Solano County. But in the Vaca they got this root louse that kills the vines. Call it phylloxera. A lot of the older vineyards have lost all their vines, and seems there's no cure for it. There's always a worm somewhere in the rose. But so far there's no sign of this louse in the Napa. Here's my son Peter. Tom you've met, and he's my youngest. Peter's second of my four sons."

Peter had a cheerful open face and gave Doc a friendly handshake. They had talked at the family meal on Doc's first visit. "I'm making my rounds to check everything," he told Doc. "Why don't you come along?"

Doc walked with him to the gray stone building, which was two stories high but built into a cutaway hill that came level with the second story on one end. The back of the building had a large one-room extension with men and machinery working on its flat roof. Doc and Peter followed a horse-drawn cart loaded with grapes up the hill's slope, which served as a runway to the flat roof.

"The big fermentation vats are directly beneath this roof," Peter said, pointing at his feet. "There's a vat beneath each of those metal skylights. When we want to fill the vat, we mount a grape-crushing machine in the skylight and load grapes into it. That machine you see working can grind a boxful of grapes, say fifty-five to sixty pounds, in seven seconds. Each machine squeezes more than six-hundred gallons of juice per day."

Doc looked at the grapes being tipped from the cart into the crusher.

Peter continued, "We add yeast to the vats and the first fermentation lasts anything from a week to more than two weeks. The liquid is then siphoned off into a clean vat, leaving the skins, debris, and sediment behind. After a second fermentation, it's aged in casks, and then siphoned off again and bottled. Anything that goes wrong at any time ruins the wine. It's a tricky business."

"What can go wrong?" Doc asked.

"In the early stages you can lose a whole vat if a wild strain of yeast gets to grow instead of the one you introduce. Some yeasts turn the juice to vinegar or make it taste bad in other ways. Easiest thing to go wrong with a bottle of wine is for it to be heated. Cold doesn't seem to affect it, but you let a bottle sit in the sun and you kill the wine. Happens sometimes when they ship it—a whole load sits out on some dock or siding in the blazing sun for days on end." He smiled. "We try to control everything, because the name Crevetti is on the label, but there's too many things beyond our control."

Doc looked him in the eye. "You expect to lose all this to the Jones brothers at $1.25 an acre?"

Peter never blinked. "Over my dead body."

"Nearly happened to your brother Tom. He was lucky he only got shot in the leg."

"Tom's a fool," Peter said with contempt. "He forgets who and what we're fighting for and runs down to the tracks with layabouts who figure they got an excuse for daylight robbery. I reckon that bullets may have taught him a lesson. You seem to have an uncommon interest in all this."

"I do?" Doc said with a look of surprise.

"Pa was saying the same thing. He told us to be straight and aboveboard with you, because we ain't got nothing to hide. But we got a lot to lose, and you—and anyone else you might know—are welcome to learn the easy way that we ain't giving one damn grape bush up. The easy way is seeing with your own two eyes. Hard way of learnin' is coming up against us for real."

"I'll keep that in mind," Doc said in a neutral tone. He knew it was hopeless to try to persuade the Crevettis he was a chance bystander. It sounded now as if they had pegged him for an interested observer right from the start. In fact his father had probably instructed Peter to have this talk with him today. Doc could see though that they hadn't been able to make up their minds who he was working for. That was understandable, Doc decided, since he himself was having trouble clarifying that.

"I like what I see of your family and your vineyard," Doc said to Peter. "Fight to keep them and I'll help all I can. But hands off the railroad."

Peter nodded. "The railroad. That's what Pa thought. Those back-stabbing bastards who run that line—"

"I know about that," Doc said. "I'm doing my best. When I know, I'll let you know."

"You want me to keep quiet about this?" Peter asked.

Doc shrugged. "I got a feeling that after today it's not going to matter much one way or the other."

Raider stood at Napa City waiting for the northbound train on its run from Vallejo up the valley. Paul Heron stood twenty yards from him, waiting for the same train. Raider had received Doc's telegram with its disguised warning to expect trouble on the evening train. He had passed the information on to Paul. This kind of trouble was easily postponed or advanced, and might as easily occur on this, the morning train, as on the evening. He guessed it would involve Willie McPhee in his role as gunfighter.

Raider cursed Doc silently. Raider had been against Doc's plan, but since the other three had been so strongly for it he had gone along with them. It was only after they had accused him of being too vain to let Willie seem faster with a gun than he, saying it was his dumb vanity that was holding back their great plan, only then had he backed down—just to show he wasn't stupid proud. Raider had two things against what they wanted to do. First, it was putting Willie McPhee, a novice Pinkerton, in more danger than he was equipped to handle through experience. Second, Raider felt hc would be humiliated; and to him it was plain horse sense, not dumb pride, that a man never takes part in something that makes him look less than he is. But they didn't see it that way....

The train was pulling in now. Its bell sounded, and the locomotive slowed and came to a stop amid great clouds of steam. Raider and Paul entered different coaches. Raider casually eyed the occupants of his car as he walked down its aisle toward a vacant seat. Farmers and ranchers who had missed the evening train the day before, salesmen on quick tours of the valley towns, men from Napa City who had business up-valley, women laden with parcels visiting married daughters or sick relatives—the people here were not hard to classify.

One man, gaunt, in his thirties, with a lantern jaw and long sideburns, and a gun on his hip, met Raider's glance with a deliberately mocking look. "You the fella the kid with pimples outdrew up in Calistoga?"

"I never did kill a kid with pimples," Raider told him friendly-like, pausing in the aisle. So far as Raider could remember, Willie McPhee wasn't troubled by pimples in any case.

"From what I hear," the man said, "you never got no chance to show the kid mercy. He outdrew you cold."

"Never believe all you hear," Raider said and moved on.

Raider sat and stared out the window. His lips twitched with fury. He was less mad at the loudmouth stranger in the coach than at Doc Weatherbee. He blamed Doc for putting him on the defensive, of making him seem vulnerable to a jeering asshole. Yet there was something more sinister than that about this man. He was no country boy talking big in order to impress his friends. Besides, he was alone and had no one to show off in front of, except strangers on a train. He hadn't spoken so everyone in the coach would hear, like a smart-ass would. He had just quietly needled Raider and sized him up. There was something premeditated about it.

So it came as no great surprise to Raider when the man ambled along the aisle of the moving train after it had left Yountville, holding onto the seat backs to steady himself in the swaying car. He settled himself in a seat directly across the aisle from Raider. When their eyes met, he gave Raider a slow crooked grin. After that he looked out the window at the passing grassland, orchards, and vineyards.

When the train began to slow on its approach to St. Helena, the man looked directly across the aisle at Raider. "I want you off the train at this stop."

Raider guffawed. "You gotta be kidding."

"Don't push me, Raider. I ain't going to hurt you if you do what I say."

"You're going to have to hurt me a lot, mister," Raider snarled, "and I still won't be doing what you say."

The man looked at him as he might have done at a disobedient child. At that moment Raider knew he could take him—the man had believed in the staged incident with Willie in Calistoga and was sure Raider's nerve had broken. All he had to do now, by his way of thinking, was press hard enough and Raider would crack.

Raider had been up against this kind of gunfighter many times before. Their total confidence in themselves and their perception of weaknesses in others were the combination that gave them the strength to trample all in their path. But this one had bought a lie in believing Raider had lost his edge. He was now riding on a confidence he never would have had if it hadn't been for that damn Calistoga incident dreamed up by that slimy eel Weatherbee.

The coach pulled to a jerky stop, and they could hear the release of pressurized steam from the locomotive valves.

People began leaving the coach, and others outside waited for them to exit before climbing aboard themselves for the short run to Calistoga, beyond which the huge bulk of Mount St. Helena put a stop to the railroad.

"If I draw on you," the man said when he saw that Raider was making no move to leave the train, as he had ordered, "I won't be as sweet-natured as that kid. I'll squeeze the trigger."

Raider sat there silent. His right hand rested on his right knee.

The man's voice was cold. He spoke carefully. "Mr. Jones in San Francisco has deputized me to look after these trains. I'm ordering you off this train."

"Your Mr. Jones don't own this railroad. I work for those who do. But I ain't ordering you on or off, 'cause I don't give a bear's scat what you do."

The man rose slowly to his feet. Raider rose too, so as not to give his opponent the advantage of the faster draw that standing provided.

Clearly the man was having some second thoughts about Raider, but he had gone too far now to back down and save face.

Passengers dropped their newspapers and packages in their hurry to remove themselves to either end of the car, away from the two dangerous types facing each other down across its aisle, gun hands hovering close to their sidearms.

Raider watched the man's eyes, and he watched Raider's. The man's eyes flickered downward for an instant. Raider drew. As Raider's right hand pulled the revolver from its holster and leveled the barrel on his adversary, his left hand reached across and brushed back the hammer while his trigger finger squeezed.

He felt the gun move in his hand, saw the flash, smelled the burnt gunpowder, heard the shot, saw the crimson rent appear in the man's left shoulder as the .44 slug tore into the muscles and snapped blood vessels.

The injured man's weapon discharged, putting a bullet in the floorboards between the two men. This seemed to revive the gun's owner, for he now hunched his left shoulder to relieve its agony, fixed his eyes on Raider, thumbed back the hammer, and raised the barrel at him.

Raider's left hand whipped across the top of his Remington and he fanned a second shot, this time blowing away the man's right temple. The man's already dead body was flung back against the train windows. Gray matter from his brain was scattered over the seats, windows and floor like discarded pieces of scrambled egg.

Women screamed and men scattered out of his way as Raider walked up the aisle of the coach. He sat in an empty seat and picked up an abandoned copy of that day's *Napa Reporter*. Normally Raider didn't bother to read newspapers, but it gave him something to do while station porters cleaned up the mess he had left behind.

Doc noted that the morning train running north was fifty minutes late out of St. Helena. He wondered what had held it up, but gave little thought to the matter since both Raider and Paul Heron were on the train and they could look out for each other as well as take care of the train. Doc would be on hand for the evening run, when they knew they would have trouble. Meanwhile he would return to his quarters and relax for a while.

Doc was staying at a rooming house at a crossroads about five miles north of the Crevetti winery. The house, a clapboard jumble of gables, balconies, bay windows, and porches, stood in fields of grass, beyond which lay harvested cornfields not yet plowed under. Orchard groves surrounded the house: cherries, peaches, pears, plums, almonds, English walnuts, figs. The fruits had all long been picked, but the trees had been identified for Doc by Mrs. Jackson, the widow who owned the place. She had bought it for a song from a rich Philadelphian who had come west with his family to play at what he termed "a frontier existence." The Philadelphian had quickly grown weary of his experiment and had taken his family on a steam yacht to sample the delights of Honolulu.

Mrs. Jackson, whose husband had been a bank manager in San Francisco, intended to stick it out. She had Chinese farmhands to work the fields, and she rented rooms by the week to those she perceived as respectable people, which did not include the Chinese. She got good work from the farmhands because she helped them send for their wives and children. The Chinese women cooked and did housework. But Mrs. Jackson had to allow that even though she was making an economic success of the place, it could grow mighty lonesome. Especially for a woman with a spotless reputation to protect and who had hitherto led a blameless life. Doc understood all that.

When the other boarders were about in the evening, Doc and she maintained perfect decorum. Fortunately Doc's medical career allowed him a little free time in the late morning and early afternoon, during which they could develop their acquaintance. The other boarders were gone all day except for Sunday, and while the Chinese might talk among themselves about Doc and Mrs. Jackson, they formed their own little community and had almost no contacts with non-Chinese. In other words, there was no danger of gossip.

Doc walked in the pleasant October sunshine among the orchard trees toward the field where Judith was grazing. As soon as the mule saw him coming, she looked wary and about to bolt. Judith had several ponies and other mules for company, and Doc noted she had begun to lose her enthusiasm for pulling a wagon. She could usually tell whether he had work in mind or was coming just to pat her neck and feed her some sugar he had taken from Mrs. Jackson's table. Doc wasn't sure how the mule did it, but this time she looked at him carefully and guessed correctly it was sugar and not work. She started being friendly toward him.

After seeing his mule, Doc walked toward the house. He could hear the notes of the piano and wondered whether he should wait where he was till she tired of playing. Doc liked music, but there were limits. Mrs. Jackson's heavy-handed renditions of simple ditties were beyond those limits. Doc decided she had already seen him through the window and thus he continued toward the house so as not to cause her offense. He even suspected she might be playing especially for him. If only he hadn't lied to her about how much her music affected him. . . .

Although Mrs. Jackson hadn't much in the way of musical abilities, she more than made up for it with other qualities. She had been widowed early—a shapely, humorous women in her late twenties who would soon find a steady mate again to warm her bed on winter nights. Her honey-colored hair was wound in coils about her head, and she moved with a sinuous ease that made a man conscious of her hips and full breasts—and made him wonder whether these movements were deliberately provocative or unconscious on her part. Doc, who was greatly interested in such matters, had decided that she made herself deliberately seductive not so much to seduce men as to make them merely desire her—and, as a result, she wouldn't feel so neglected and alone.

It was purely out of kindness and the goodness of Doc's heart that, in spite of his business responsibilities, he took time off to provide her with much-needed male companionship. Doc knew the only way to put a stop to her piano playing was to approach her from behind, listen respectfully for a minute while caressing her back, and then reach around beneath her flailing arms to hold her full breasts—hold them firmly, squeeze their resilient softness in his palms, feel the nipples come erect beneath his fingertips. . . . The piano notes grew softer, became less frequent, and at last died away altogether.

Doc unbuttoned her bodice and reached in beneath her lace underthings to fondle the globes of her breasts. His finger traced circles on the areolae of her nipples. Then, bending over her, he playfully nipped on the tender erectile tissue of the nipples themselves, causing them to grow yet harder and stand out more firmly.

"Someone will walk in on us here," Mrs. Jackson murmured.

Having chastely removed his hands and recovered her

bosom, she rose from the piano stool and headed for the staircase. Doc followed in her wake.

She had lost her shyness in disrobing before him, and now she eagerly displayed her body before his eyes, removing garment after garment, exposing a little more of herself with each movement.

She stood still while he ran his hands over her body in soft little caresses and strokes that sent sensual shivers through her flesh. Still fully clothed, Doc lavished attention on her statuesque naked form with his tongue. Its moist tip traced arcs and arabesques across her smooth, flawless skin. She grew increasingly agitated, clasped his head in both her hands, and pressed his tongue into places of particular delicacy—finally standing with her legs apart and letting his tongue lap over and sneak inside the opening of her inner joy.

She pulled him toward her bed, feverishly tugging on his clothes to get them off his body. It wasn't long before he took pleasure in the warm silky feel of her body against his. He stroked and fondled her till she no longer knew who or where she was, until she was a mass of melting sensations crying out to him to ease her heat.

She lay on her back, heaving with passion, legs parted submissively. He pressed his distended cock between the lips of her sex, and felt his great knob be hungrily sucked in by her moist throbbing cunt.

He drove his rod deep within her—heard her answering gasp, felt the tightening pulse of her furnished vagina close around his dick. He withdrew to the very tip of his prick and then thrust its full length forward into her parting quivering clutching tissues. Doc rode and plunged, rode and plunged, filling her needful want with the mastery of his cock.

CHAPTER SIX

Tod Jones swung his silver-tipped cane in what he imagined was a cosmopolitan man-about-town manner, except there was something about the way he held the cane that made it clear he would have been equally comfortable holding a cudgel. His bullet head, massive jaws, great gnarled hands, and barrel chest in a stocky body never seemed fully contained by the somber banker's suit he always wore. Tod Jones took care to greet anyone who glanced at him, lifted his hat to the ladies, smiled at babies, and patted the heads of children. Everyone said he could have been mayor of San Francisco if he wanted to. Instead he was holding out for a U.S. Senate seat in the election next month. In the meantime he was showing himself to the voters.

Tod lived with his wife and children in a relatively modest mansion near the base of Nob Hill, though he could easily have afforded to build himself a palace higher up the hill with the cream of society. But Tod knew he had to protect his image as a man of the people if he was to get their votes. He knew well that a politician weakens himself when he becomes too closely associated with the flagrantly wealthy and snobbish—the trouble being that there aren't enough of the very rich to vote a man into power. Once a politician was identified with the millionaires, even if he was not one himself, it was assumed by the public that he was a lackey who did their bidding. Tod's trick was to hide his millions and be just plain folks like the man on the street who was going to vote for him, he hoped.

Even his enemies admitted that Tod Jones had a lot of horse sense. His wife was a fool. His sons and daughters were fools. But more important, his brother was a fool. General opinion had it that without this albatross of a brother hanging around his neck, Tod Jones would have been on Capitol Hill long ago, hobnobbing with the likes of General Grant and Mr. Hamilton Fish and making fine deals for himself, with hopefully a little spillover or trickledown for the people of San Francisco. No one in the city had too many illusions about the men they sent to Washington, D.C.

Tod and his brother, Harry Jones, often had a good laugh at the idea of Harry holding back the career of his respectable brother. But they saw that this game worked well for them both, and they each played to the hilt the roles expected of them.

Tod walked purposefully with his cane down to the docks, where he knew he would find his brother at this hour. His expression was filled with righteous indignation, and to any stranger it would be instantly clear that here was a righteous and indignant man off to set some wrong to right and reprimand some morally reprehensible scoundrel in the process.

It was early afternoon, and the sun had scorched off the last of the morning's fog. The salt tang in the air grew stronger by the minute as he neared the docks. He could see the mast tips of the schooners nodding in threes above the roofs of the waterside warehouses.

Tod walked into a countinghouse on the street level of a huge warehouse and looked around among the men transacting business. Not finding who he wanted, he wandered back amid the stacked merchandise. In one corner, beneath a grimy window, four men sat on casks and played cards on a fifth cask set between them. One of the four was Tod's identical twin, Harry. Though they were now forty-six years old, they still preserved the very close resemblance to each other they had shared as children. While Tod dressed in dark clothes that would have been no disgrace to the strictest clergyman, Harry wore a loud red check suit, a burgundy vest, a brown bicycling cap, and a derringer in a holster attached to his yellow suspenders. He was in the middle of telling a joke about a sex-starved Chinaman when he noticed his brother's approach. He stopped in mid-sentence, threw his cards down, and waved his three companions away. They too had spotted Tod coming and hurried away willingly.

"Good morning, brother," Tod greeted Harry civilly.

"Yeah," Harry said noncommittally.

Tod drew a telegram from his pocket. "This just arrived. Let me read it to you. 'An unidentified man who was heard to claim he worked for Mr. Jones of San Francisco and was sent by him to protect trains in the Napa Valley died today of gunshot wounds inflicted by a railroad guard at St. Helena. Await instructions. Bingham.' I assume you agree that I respond to this Bingham by denying all knowledge of the affair and by suggesting the telegram was addressed to some other Jones than me."

"Bingham's a lawyer in St. Helena, a good man," Harry said, his eyes almost closed and his mind obviously on something other than Bingham's excellence. "Sure, you know nothing about it. Neither do I. What do they want me to do? I ain't going to pay to give the bum a decent burial."

Tod's face was grim. "You sent a gunslinger on that train after we agreed to play things down so far as the railroad was concerned?"

"I had to send him. The railroad hired some kind of a joke that a kid outdrew and didn't bother to kill because he's harmless."

"I thought they hired Pinkertons," Tod said.

"That was the rumor. But this one didn't sound like no Pinkerton."

"He killed the man you sent."

Harry spat. "Probably shot him in the back."

"I still can't see why you sent this man, Harry. This new security man the railroad has—aren't there two of them?—shot two squatters, and the trouble on the railroad died down. Isn't that what we want?"

"It *was* what we wanted, but no longer," Harry said. He paused to light a cigar. "You take care of things in Washington and leave local matters to me."

"Harry, I have to know what you're doing."

"All right. Way I figure it is we were wrong to think quieting things down on the railroad would be in our favor. Look what happened. First off, everyone was on the squatters' side and calling us names. Then the squatters started stopping trains and those people got theirselves killed. People began to see the squatters as the bad guys and said they deserved whatever they had coming to them. That's the attitude we have to keep alive. I aim to stir up a mess of trouble out that way by any means I can. If they have to bring in the U.S. cavalry to restore order, it will be in our favor."

Tod looked doubtful. "What will the newspapers print about me for the voters to read?"

"I'll look after that," Harry reassured him. "It just needs explaining that you're a victim—me too—of these violent land-grabbing whoreson squatters who had best be gotten rid of as a danger to the progress of society in these parts."

Tod looked happier. "You know, the attitude in Washington is deep concern over the interruption of train service and communications—the land-grant thing has already been forgotten. If you can make it look like the squatters are interfering with federal and state communications, no matter what their cause the authorities will be against them."

Harry winked. "Now you're coming around to seeing it my way."

Tod smiled. "I always was a bit slower than you, Harry."

"Main thing is folks think you're the smart and honest one."

Tod placed his hand over his heart, and they both laughed.

Willie McPhee looked at the three other men, and from time to time they looked at him. There was nothing even faintly resembling trust between them and him. At one point one had said to him, "If we get nothing out of this, neither will you." He was referring to Willie's pay being a share of the loot. Willie had only nodded that he understood.

All four of them waited crouched in low brush by the railroad tracks just north of the town of St. Helena. It would be one man per passenger coach, with Willie taking the one Raider always rode on, the second car. Paul Heron always rode in the first car. If Raider was not in the second car, it would be up to Willie to locate him in one of the others before things got under way. This might be a problem, since the passenger cars were not interconnected.

The two men who were to take the third and fourth coaches were a bit jumpy in case one of them would pick Raider.

One said in a bitter joke, "Willie, you won't have no trouble finding Raider on the train if he ain't in the second car. You'll be able to hear him shootin' the shit out of us."

From where they were they would be able to hear the train pulling into the station at St. Helena, stop, and then build up steam and start off toward them. They would be able to jump aboard quite easily before the locomotive built up speed.

Willie tried talking to pass the time while they waited for the train to show. "I make a living from my gun, that's why I'm here. I got no land like you have. If I had land to work, even as a squatter, you sure wouldn't find me here."

"You don't look like no gunfighter to me," one said guardedly.

Willie grinned. "That's why I'm still alive. I don't look

the part, so I take 'em by surprise."

"We ain't squatters," another said. "We're just low-downers from the hills."

"What's low-downers?" Willie asked.

"Poor whites, 'cept we don't like to be called that by no one 'cept one of our own. Low-downer ain't much of a compliment neither."

The others laughed.

Willie nodded sympathetically. "You do a little rustling, a little road agenting now and then, hire out as a gun?"

"Nah. More like we steal a pig than a cow. And being a road agent ain't something I'd recommend round here—it's a dangerous occupation. You're likely to get your ass shot off by the man you're trying to hold up. And we ain't no hired guns, that's for sure."

"Then what do you think is going on here?" Willie asked.

"Like you, we get a share of the loot. Maybe a little more besides. Take it back into the hills with us."

"All three of us and our families live in this here abandoned mining town."

"Shut your mouth, Chad."

"Willie ain't going to say nothing to nobody, is you, Willie?"

"Hell, no," Willie said.

"You may be all right, Willie, I ain't saying you ain't. I'm just telling Chad here to stop running his mouth off."

They were quiet for a spell after that.

The bell of the train sounded as it neared the station at St. Helena, and they all tensed up. After a few minutes they heard the chuffing of the locomotive as it pulled out of the station. The rails next to them hummed with sound. The four men spread apart, with slightly more than the length of a railroad coach between them, and ducked back into the shrubbery alongside the tracks. They emerged simultaneously from hiding when the locomotive passed the northernmost man, ran beside the moving cars, and pulled themselves aboard by clutching the brass rails at the car doors.

Willie climbed the steps into the swaying car and was met by Raider, gun in hand, in the aisle.

Raider jerked a thumb over his shoulder. "Go help Paul in the first car. I'll take care of things down this end. How many are back this way?"

"Two."

Raider headed for the door. To get from one car to another, they had to lean out the door of the moving train, hanging on to the rear brass rail, and reach around to grab the brakeman's ladder to the roof on the outside rear of the car. For one precarious moment, each of them, one after the other, hung by one hand to a ladder rung as his body swung above the clattering wheels on the steel rails.

When he reached the car roof, Raider jumped back over the space to the car behind. Willie ran forward along the roof of the second car. The wind swept against him, and he had to crouch into it as he ran to maintain his balance. When he reached the forward end of the car, he threw himself into a huge leap that he thought would land him six feet clear onto the roof of the first car. With the headwind against him and the cars moving beneath him as he leaped, he landed almost on the rear edge of the first car's roof, teetered a moment on one foot, and almost feel backward down between the cars of the now speeding train.

Willie regained his balance and steadied himself on the roof, which now pitched sharply from side to side as the train rounded a curve. Rows of vines grew on each side of the tracks, and up ahead he could see Mount St. Helena, with its bare top and tree-fringed slopes and spurs. The hills all about looked blue in the distance.

This is one hell of a time to stop to admire the scenery. Willie said to himself and climbed down the brakeman's ladder. Since the valley was level throughout its length, no brakemen were needed to ride atop the cars. At the bottom of the ladder, he reversed the procedure he and Raider had performed before, this time reaching around to clutch the brass rail and swinging into the doorway of the car.

The low-downer named Chad was at the other end of the

car, gun in hand and a wild look on his face. Willie drew his revolver and walked down the aisle toward him. The passengers were sitting scared and quiet. Chad smiled with relief at Willie's approach.

"You take care of Raider?"

Willie nodded.

"So far no trouble here," Chad said. "I know one of these people is the railroad security agent, but I ain't sure which one. You think it's that fat one in the third seat to the right?"

The fat man in the third seat to the right looked up in alarm when he heard Chad say this in his loud careless voice. It was Paul Heron.

"No, I don't think so," Willie said, equally loudly. "He looks too soft and flabby for the job."

"I don't care how he looks," Chad complained. "He keeps eyeing me like he means trouble. Likely every man in this car is armed to the teeth, and I was standing here all alone before you came. This ain't my line of work. Never done nothing like this before, and I won't again. I tell you, Willie, I don't like it at all. If I could walk out of it this moment, I would."

Willie gestured to the car doorway, through which they could see the countryside passing. "We've slowed some in the last minute. If you want out, go now."

Chad gave him a toothless smile and shook his hand. Without another word, he holstered his gun, went down the steps, and leaped out.

Raider swung in the door of the third car and slapped leather. The low-downer was in the middle of the car, shouting at a passenger and threatening him with his revolver. Raider stayed where he was at the end of the car till the bandit noticed him. He moved his gun from the passenger's forehead and made to point it at Raider. Raider gently squeezed the Remington's trigger. He couldn't risk hitting any of the passengers—it had to be a deadeye shot—and pulling on the trigger hard might have spoiled his aim. His left hand held his right wrist steady, he stood with his feet apart for perfect balance, his right forefinger squeezing gently on the curved metal trigger. . . .

The bandit roared and scratched his fingers across his chest, trying to pluck out the knot of pain. His revolver clattered harmlessly to the floor, and his eyes rolled in his head as he roared once more and scratched at his chest. Raider left him to it and went out the way he came in.

Raider climbed the brakeman's ladder, ran the length of the third car on its narrow pitching roof, and jumped onto the fourth car, the last of the passenger coaches before the boxcars. He descended its ladder and swung himself by the brass rail into its forward doorway. The gunsel saw him right off and took cover behind an occupied seat at the other end of the car. Raider couldn't fire for fear of hitting innocent travelers. He knew his opponent would have no such scruples.

Up to this point the passengers had been reasonably sure they wouldn't be harmed or robbed if they sat quiet. But none of them were foolish enough to believe they were safe trapped in a moving railroad car with two pistoleros on the point of fighting it out.

Raider had begun to back off toward the door, covering his retreat with his gun, with the intention of settling this some other way at a later time, when an elderly gentleman with a dignified bearing and a neatly grimmed mustache leaped to his feet.

"Damn you, sir," he shouted at Raider. "How dare you engage in gunplay in the presence of women and children?"

He slashed down with his heavy cane on Raider's hand, and its brass knob caught Raider's knuckles, knocking the gun from his hand.

"You crazy old bastard!" Raider yelled.

The gunsel at the other end of the car fired, and the bullet lodged in the wood endwall behind Raider. He scooped his revolver up off the floor and slipped it in its holster. The gunsel fired again. The old boy with the brass-knobbed cane collapsed on top of Raider with a groan. Raider scrambled for the door as he saw the low-downer running up the aisle toward him. Raider had hardly any feeling in his right hand; he couldn't close it into a fist, and he couldn't shoot left-handed worth a damn.

Raider hung on to the brass rail with the crook of his right elbow as he swung around to grab the brakeman's ladder with his left hand. When his feet missed the ladder's bottom rung, he hung suspended between the cars by his left hand on an upper rung. He hugged the ladder to him with his right arm and found the bottom rung with his knees.

As he knelt there an instant, saved from the slicing steel of the wheels and rails, he expected to see a gun barrel and a head angle around the end of the car to pick him off like a rat in a barrel. The low-downer had stopped to reload, having spent only two cartridges. And had missed his opportunity. Raider wasn't going to give him another one.

He clambered up the ladder onto the roof of the car. He saw Willie in the act of jumping from the roof of the second car back to that of the third. After Willie landed and ran closer, Raider gestured to him, pointing first to his own injured hand and then down between the cars from where he expected the gunsel to appear at any moment up the ladder in pursuit. The shit knew Raider was hurt, and maybe knew who he was, too, and wanted to put a notch on his gun by the name of Raider. Otherwise he'd be a wise man and stay below in the car.

The crown of the gunsel's hat showed as he climbed up the ladder. Before his eyes reached roof level and saw Raider, Willie McPhee fired from behind him and whipped the hat off the gunsel's head. The hat blew by the side of the train for a moment before being sucked in on the rails beneath the wheels.

The bullet, having passed neatly through the crown of the hat, snicked off the metalwork rim of the car roof and touched the sleeve of Raider's jacket—what felt to him like a light and casual touch but one which left an angry furrow in the leather. Raider dropped to his belly on the car roof and hoped Willie had seen the danger of firing with him immediately behind the intended target. Raider had no time to wave a warning to Willie because the gunsel's head reappeared above the level of the car roofs. but this time, though he was clinging to the ladder, which would have brought him literally face to face with Raider, who was lying on the roof only a foot away, he had his head twisted about to see Willie behind him and return his fire. As the gunsel brought his pistol to bear on Willie, Raider rapped him across the back of the head with the knuckles of his left fist.

The gunsel fell down between the cars onto the rails beneath. The tonnage of the rolling stock, borne on the narrow wheels, sliced through his meat and bones, successive wheels chopping his remains into yet smaller pieces, till all that was left on the roadbed after the train passed over was scattered carrion for buzzards and coyotes, splintered bones that would dry in the sun.

Doc Weatherbee had tied his horse to a bush almost a mile back, and now he kept to the deep cover of the shrubs. Nine or ten men stood alongside the railroad tracks, all of them armed with rifles or shotguns, talking and smoking—waiting there as easy as if they were standing at a station like any legitimate passengers. Two wagon teams and their saddle horses were hitched in the shade of a clump of trees a few hundred yards back. Doc found himself a hiding place in a thick patch of lilac, about halfway between the men and their horses. When they left, this was the way they would come.

So far as Doc could see, there were no rails lifted or blockades of any sort, which surprised him, since he had no way of knowing that the waiting men expected their four colleagues who had boarded the train to force it to a stop at this place. Doc heard the train approach from a long distance off. He checked his Winchester repeater and his Diamondback .38 pistol. Although Doc rarely carried arms, he readily acknowledged there were some situations in which a man could not get by without them. He had guessed that today would be one of those situations.

The train came. It slowed some before it reached the men, as if it were preparing to stop, then two men jumped from it and the train picked up speed again. Doc recognized Raider and Willie McPhee as the two who had jumped off the train. So did the men waiting beside the tracks. They did nothing for a moment till they saw that the train was going to keep moving. They fired into the locomotive cabin as it passed them. Raider and Willie fired their revolvers at the men, who moved to cover and shot back at them, allowing the train to go by without being attacked further.

Raider and Willie's two pistols were no match for the rifles of the men. Doc had to do something. He ran in a crouch to where the horses were hitched and looked back to make sure he hadn't been seen. The horses' owners were too busy concentrating on shooting up Raider and Willie, whom they regarded as a traitor to their side. Doc unhooked the harness traces from the wagons and raised the empty shafts. He untied the saddle horses. Then, as the horses stood nervously about, he lined up the sights of his Winchester on the back of one of the gang. His aim was true. When he squeezed the trigger, the man jumped up as if something had bit him from behind—as it most surely had.

The horses bolted, panicked by the shot. Doc ran through the bushes and shrubs and loosed off a couple of shots from another position. Then three revolver shots. He changed position and fired again. He emptied the seventeen rounds in the magazine of the Winchester and the six in the Diamondback .38, firing wildly most of the time, intent only on staying completely out of sight and creating the impression that three or four guns were firing from different positions.

Seeing their horses bolting would probably have been enough to unnerve the men down by the tracks. They quit their extermination drive on Willie and Raider and began to think about saving their own hides. But not before Doc had picked off a second man with one of his wild shots from the hip. The bullet caught the man in the ribs, and he rolled round and round in the dust, hollering and screaming.

The sight and sound of their injured comrade was more than enough to fully convince any of those who might have been wavering about wanting to stay or run. They left him to die, twisting in the dust, and took off in every direction through the bushes and trees.

CHAPTER SEVEN

"I ain't going back on that stupid little train, Doc," Raider said with feeling. "If I ride up and down on that damn thing one more time, I'll go crazy. I'll run amuck. You'll read this in the newspaper: 'Pinkerton runs train into San Pablo Bay. Said he wanted to see if it would float.' You'd have to come after me, Doc, and bring me to justice."

"A pleasure," Doc assured him.

"You think you could?" Raider taunted.

"No problem."

Raider poked his finger in Doc's chest. "You have the nerve to say it to my face that you could bring me in if you had to?"

"Why not?" Doc responded. "I heard a kid outdrew you in Calistoga and an old man with a cane disarmed you on the train."

Raider glanced at the back of his hand. "Shit. That old bastard just happened to touch some kind of nerve. That hand was paralyzed for more than ten minutes. Though it was working fine, just as if nothing happened, by the time

I jumped off the train." Finally Raider saw the humor in the situation and laughed. Then he was grim again. "That old guy on the train may have been half crazy to attack me with his cane, but I was there to protect him and I lost him. It's my fault he got killed. I don't like that happening to someone in my care, even if he is nuts and attacks me instead of them."

"He was confused," Doc told Raider. "His family says so, and no one blames you except yourself. You did what you could. We can put Willie on the train with Paul. All right, Willie?"

"Sure." Willie was still pleased to do as he was told.

Raider brightened. "I'm going to get me a horse and ride the country awhile, even if the place is all shot to hell with these little grape plants."

The town of Calistoga was only a main street at right angles to where the road and railroad came in side by side. They heard the train bell and then the locomotive puffing into the town, to the end of the line. It would only take Paul Heron a few minutes to come from the train to Cheeseborough's, the hotel at which they sat and talked. When Paul arrived, he greeted them cheerfully and produced a Western Union telegram addressed to Doc. He then flopped his bulk down in an easy chair and poured himself a cup of coffee.

Purpose of your assignment is to protect lives of those aboard trains and railroad property. Railroad company is not directly involved in land disputes. Neither should you be.

Wagner

Doc sighed and threw the telegram on the table for the others to see.

Raider's reaction was typical of him. "Serves you dumb bastards right for putting too much of the truth into your reports to those housebound turkeys in Chicago. You cut back your reports to a few essentials, and then you won't get interferin' communications such as this."

Doc said, "Note what Wagner actually says. He doesn't tell us not to get involved. He just said we shouldn't. I interpret that as his leaving things to our own judgment."

"Damn right," Raider agreed.

"That's nonsense," Willie McPhee said indignantly. "Headquarters' intentions are perfectly clear; that we restrict ourselves—" Willie broke off as he felt Raider's powerful hand descend upon his shoulder, friendly as an eagle's talon.

"You heard what Doc said, Willie," Raider growled. "Chicago is leaving things so we can judge for ourselves. Now, I got no objection to that. Do you?"

"I guess not, Raider." Willie shook his shoulder free.

Paul Heron smiled. "It seems a shame to allow a decent young operative like Willie out in the field with a pair of bums like you two. Don't let them push you around, kid."

"You going to listen to this tub of lard?" Raider asked Willie.

Willie knew he had been intimidated and had the grace not to try to pretend otherwise.

"One thing the telegram states is true," Doc said, businesslike as usual. "The railroad company is not directly involved in the land disputes. The only reason trains are being attacked is because they make easier targets than the people involved in the dispute. If the squatters go into San Francisco, they find themselves on the Jones brothers' turf. And if the Jones brothers come out to the Prospect ranch, they find the squatters have the upper hand. What we have achieved so far is to make the railroad a less easy target than it has been. What's the result of that going to be? Both sides are going to start looking for new targets."

"Each other," Willie suggested.

"If you and Paul keep the trains protected, that's what will happen," Doc said. "In the meantime Raider and I will have time to look into some other things. I think it's to our advantage now to have it known we're Pinkertons. I'm sure word is out on that already."

"It is," Paul confirmed. "One of the newspapers found out."

"Chicago had its chance to pull us out of here before we got too deep in the mud," Doc said philosophically. "Looks like we're going to have to wade right in now."

As they listened to what Doc said about wading into mud, they looked at his dandy's fresh-pressed clothes and laughed.

Tod Jones's wife drew her lips taut and nodded coldly to her brother-in-law, Harry. The very sight of him in his vulgar clothes, sprawled at his ease on the furniture of her drawing room, a big black cigar reeking in his mouth, spitting in the fireplace, made her tremble with rage. Her husband and Harry had been talking about politics, and of course stopped the moment she entered the room. At first she had thought politics would be good for Tod—at least the Senate would remove him three thousand miles from that ogre Harry, but lately she had come to see that, as in all things, the twin brothers were in this together too. Once she had even heard Harry laughingly boast how, with a brother on each coast, they could squeeze America between them. She ordered tea and chatted about inconsequential things. She quickly gave up and left them to their cigars, bourbon, and politics.

"Run for the seat on credit," Harry told Tod, picking up the conversation at the point where his sister-in-law had interrupted it twenty minutes before. "When you're sitting in the U.S. Senate, you can pay them back twice over in favors. Don't they know that?"

"I've done all that, Harry. But I'm going to have to buy votes to get elected. And I can't do that on credit."

Harry began, "I'll raise cash down on the docks—"

"I've already included what you can raise by thieving and arm-twisting on the waterfront," Tod told him. "Now we have all that real estate just lying there in the Napa Valley if we could get even some of those damn squatters off it. Up till now, Harry, we haven't been pressured by time. We've been in no great hurry to remove them. We no longer have that luxury, because we have to show the money men that we are *capable* of evicting these squatters before they will deal with us seriously. If we can prove our strength and determination to the banks by driving off some of the squatters and keeping them off, I'll have financiers knocking on my door with bags of greenbacks. But we must watch out for one thing: my political reputation."

Harry said, "You mean *I* gotta do the dirty work."

Tod nodded.

"I'd be mighty pleased to run them egg-suckin' squatters into the ocean," Harry said. "Remember, the only thing that's been holding me back is what your precious voters will think of you." He grinned. "I guess that now since you're buying their votes, it doesn't matter what they think."

"That's about it," Tod agreed. "My helpers claim that no one in his right mind will vote for me unless he gets at least a meal and a glass of whiskey out of it."

"I'd even think twice about it then if I wasn't your brother," Harry said and guffawed. "Out in the Napa, things might work real easy if I can light a fire under those Crevettis. Old Enrico has about four hundred acres, his sons between them hold another two hundred, and his cousins and in-laws are squatting their fat asses on, say, another four hundred acres. Call it a thousand acres that Enrico and his family control. The Prospect ranch is five thousand, so they hold one-fifth of it. All the other homesteaders are small holders, and they're divided, and some don't speak to the others—you know how it goes. Only the Crevetti family, with that winery, is making a lot of money. The others are mostly poor. A lot don't read or write. They won't have any comeback against us once the Crevettis are gone."

"How will you get rid of them?" Tod asked.

"Cause trouble all around them. They'll destroy themselves. You'll see. When we get to sell all that land in forty-acre lots, we'll be as rich as any man in California.

If you do well in the Senate, Tod, maybe you'll be President one day. I hope when and if that happens, you don't forget the brother you left back here in San Francisco."

"I'll never forget what I owe you, Harry," Tod said with tears of emotion glistening in his eyes at the thought of his future career in Washington.

The two city gents consulted a sheaf of papers, looked at the small frame house, and marked its location on a map. They left their horse and buggy on the roadside and walked up to the house.

"Your father here, sonny?" one of them asked a ten-year-old scattering a bucket of cornmeal about the yard for the hens.

"I dunno."

The man gave the boy a nickel and a business card. "Go get him for me."

The boy stood and read the card.

"Hurry along," the man told him.

But the boy wanted to show off his school learning. He read aloud slowly, "'Russel and Gibbs, Surveyors and Land Agents, San Francisco.' That right? You be Mr. Russel and Mr. Gibbs?"

"No. They own the firm; we work for them. Now go find your father. We can't spend all day here."

The boy's father was in the barn behind the frame house. When his son read the business card to him, he took down an old single-barrel shotgun from pegs on the wall, searched around on a shelf till he found a badly made cartridge, and loaded it in the barrel.

"You take that card to old Mr. Crevetti or one of his sons," he told his boy. "Ride over there like the wind. Meantime I'll drive those two critters off my spread."

The boy didn't bother with a saddle. He placed the bit in the pony's mouth, pulled the bridle over its head, and stood on a wood rail to climb on the animal's back. He cracked his hand on the pony's rump and cantered beneath the line of trees leading down to the road. Looking over his shoulder, he saw the two men who worked for Russel and Gibbs backing away from his father's leveled gun. One was holding out papers to his father as he retreated. The boy smiled. Papers with writing on them weren't going to take that dude far with his father.

When the boy reached the Crevetti winery, he knew he would find old Enrico lurking about the vats somewhere, worrying that his sons weren't doing things right. He found the old man talking with his oldest son, Henry. They listened to what the boy had to say.

"Your father mustn't do anything they tell him to," Henry said urgently.

"Didn't look like he was about to," the boy said proudly.

Henry rushed away, red in the face and eyes blazing.

Old Enrico said to the boy, "You go down straightaway to the widow Jackson's and show that card to those two Pinkertons staying there. Tell them there's bound to be trouble. If Weatherbee and Raider aren't there, find them. I'll send some lads here after my son Henry."

The boy nodded self-importantly and ran to his pony. Enrico looked after him as he scrambled onto the animal's back and after his oldest son, who was raising a plume of dust as he urged his mount out of sight along the road. Enrico stood in envy of their youth and vigor for a moment, remembering all he had been once upon a time. Then he shambled off to find others to go after Henry.

Carver and Cale were showing the back roads of the Prospect ranch to the four men Harry Jones had sent out from San Francisco. Neither much relished the job of showing these four no-good drifters about this part of the Napa, but they didn't have much choice since Harry Jones had sent the four to Carver's spread and the men had asked for them both by name. Cale and Carver had both signed entitlements with the Jones brothers which gave them their land for the payment of only $10 per acre—Carver had eighty acres, and Cale fifty. What neither of them had reckoned on was that they would have to raise the money by a fixed date, Carver $800 and Cale $500, or lose the land. Their farms gave them little more than subsistence, and neither had any other source of cash or any money in the bank. So they jumped at Harry Jones's offer to do tasks at his bidding for big write-offs of their cash debts. Harry was generous. There was almost nothing Carver and Cale wouldn't do for him.

The six men were riding along a lonely stretch of road when a lone horseman approached them in a hurry.

"That's Henry Crevetti, Enrico's oldest son," Carver shouted.

"The winery owner's son?" one of the drifters asked.

Carver nodded.

"You and Cale get lost awhile so he don't know you," the drifter said. "We want to talk with him."

Carver followed Cale off the road into a hollow filled with oaks and high brush, hoping Henry hadn't already recognized them.

The four riders met Henry on the road and held up their hands for him to stop. He was armed, as they were, but no man made a move for his gun. They faced him in the roadway, four on one, the horses pulling at their reins and taking small steps to the side.

The leader of the drifters shouted, "You know this here is the Prospect ranch?"

"I was born here," Henry Crevetti said coldly.

"I don't care where you was born. You're trespassin' here by law."

"That's none of your concern," Henry said shortly.

"That's not how I look on it," the drifter went on. "Breaking the law is a real source of concern to me. Seems you ain't nothin' but a common outlaw who should be on a 'Wanted' poster." He bared his green fangs in a watery smile. "Maybe we could even collect a bounty on you."

"I'm a law-abiding man," Henry said. "It's those who hired you are the real outlaws. They think they can get anything they want by corrupting others. They'll find themselves up against a stone wall out here in Napa."

The drifter looked about him. "I don't see no stone wall."

Henry pounded himself on the chest, his anger rising. "I'm that stone wall! Go tell your employer that!"

He never saw how one of the drifters, a man who hadn't said a word, eased a Colt from its holster. The gun roared and the .45 bullet struck Henry Crevetti just to the right of his nose, shattering his cheekbone and entering his cranial cavity from below. Henry slipped sideways out of the saddle and was dead before he hit the road.

The leader didn't turn around to face the man who had fired the shot. He asked slowly, "What made you do that?"

"I didn't like his face."

All three of the younger Crevetti brothers—Ernest, Peter, and Tom—rode hard and fast after their oldest brother. By the time their father had collected them at various parts of the winery and they had fetched their guns and saddled up, Henry had a twenty-minute lead on them. They hurried because they knew Henry wouldn't back down from anyone, even if he was alone, and that could mean bad trouble from land agents sent by the Jones brothers.

They saw two men approach in a buggy and slowed to take a look at them. The men, both city types, looked nervous, said nothing, and seemed in a hurry to move along. The brothers smiled at one another.

"Looks as if Henry put his boot to their butts," Tom said. "Sure didn't take him long to get those boys moving out of here."

Half a mile farther on they found Henry's body by the side of the road. He was lying on his back on some pastureland, with half his face stove in by the bullet and his blood drying on the grass. His horse stood grazing twenty feet away.

The three looked down from the saddle at the remains of their oldest brother. They were too shocked to speak or do anything. Finally Tom and Peter turned to Ernest. He was the oldest now.

"You got your leg shot up, Tom," Ernest said. "Stay with him." He nodded to Peter and they galloped back the way they had come.

As soon as they had gone, Tom burst into tears, climbed down out of the saddle, and hugged the body of his dead brother.

For Ernest and Peter, there was no time for tears. Their horses were fresh, and they raised a big cloud of dust behind them as they galloped abreast full out along the road. A single horse pulling a buggy loaded with two grown men could not stay long ahead of them, and two strangers from the city were not going to lose two local boys who knew every track and byway off the road. From time to time they could see the ruts made by the buggy wheels in soft sandy stretches of the road.

When at last they caught sight of the vehicle, they saw that its riders were hightailing it out of the valley as fast as they could. Any doubt Ernest and Peter might have had before this was gone now. These men had murdered their brother and were now hoping to escape without paying for it. The two brothers galloped level with the buggy, one on each side of it, and poked the barrels of their .45s in the earholes of the city gents, who now thought it best to slow their four-wheel carriage.

"We represent Russell and Gibbs," the driver of the buggy said in affronted tones. He fished out a business card. Ernest refused it.

"You work for Tod and Harry Jones?" Peter asked.

"Not directly," the man explained. "You see, Russell and Gibbs are surveyors and land agents—"

"Who hired you?" Peter asked impatiently.

"Well, Mr. Harry Jones retained the services of our company—"

"The Jones brothers sent 'em," Peter said to Ernest.

"I thought so," Ernest said shortly. "You didn't happen to see a body on the side of the road back there?" he asked the buggy driver.

"No, we saw nothing," the man said a mite too quickly.

Ernest said quietly, "I don't believe you." He holstered his gun, pulled two rawhide thongs from his saddle, and jumped from his horse aboard the buggy while his brother kept the two men covered.

"We don't even have guns," the second man whined.

"You won't be needing any," Ernest said, tying the man's hands behind him with a thong. "You boys have done all the shootin' today you'll ever do again."

"We saw him! I admit it! I lied to you!" The driver of the buggy suddenly grew voluble as he felt his wrists being cut with rawhide. "I thought it best to keep going. We'd just been run off one farm at the end of a shotgun. We hadn't been told to expect anything like this. I swear it to you! He was just lying there when we saw him...." His voice trailed off as he realized their two abductors were not even listening to him.

Ernest remounted and reached down for the head of the horse harnessed to the buggy. He led the animal by the reins, and the two captive land agents bounced on the bench seat, hands tied behind them, trying to look more indignant than worried. Now and then one or other of them would try to strike up a conversation with Ernest, but he was no talker. Peter rode behind the buggy, fussing with a lariat.

Ernest stopped the buggy where a grove of oaks grew at a right angle to the road. The nearest tree stretched a thick branch out over the roadway. Peter threw his lariat over it, and its free end, tied in a noose, swung to and fro before the men's faces. Ernest slipped the noose over one man's head and tightened it around his neck. Peter dismounted, pulled the rope taut, and tied it to the base of the tree.

The second land agent tried to roll from the high buggy seat into the roadway, but Ernest beat him with the butt of his Winchester till the man sat back beside his partner again, blood streaming from his nose, down his vest, and onto his pant legs. Peter tied a noose in Ernest's lariat, flipped it over the bough, waited till the noose was fitted, tautened the rope, and tied it down.

Both the land agents were babbling explanations. Peter

nodded to Ernest. Ernest cracked an oak branch on the back of the horse between the shafts, and the buggy lurched forward.

The land agents performed their dance of death, side by side, in midair above the roadway. Ernest and Peter watched and waited till all their kicking stopped after a few minutes. They left them swinging there and rode back to help Tom with the body of their brother.

The priest finished the graveside prayers, and the crowd of mourners moved slowly out of the graveyard. Henry Crevetti had been just like his father, and he would be sorely missed. People remembered when he had done nice things for old people, acts of charity, funny things he had done as a child. No one mentioned that Henry had already killed three men in separate gunfights, that he liked to disappear for days on end several times a year—his wife used to accuse him of going to the sin palaces of San Francisco. He would be sorely missed by all the family. Lord grant him peace.

It was true enough he would be sorely missed by all the family. Henry had been very much the son and heir and oldest brother. The others had always deferred to him willingly. Old Enrico had surrendered the family leadership without a struggle to his oldest son. Everyone knew the old man's complaints were not meant to be taken seriously.

On this day of his brother's funeral, Ernest found himself being deferred to by all his relatives, in-laws, and friends. Those who had once treated him as an equal now dealt with him with careful respect. He would have to earn their allegiance—or their open disrespect—by his future actions. They would give him time to prove himself. In the meantime Ernest found himself in the uncomfortable position of grieving for his dead brother and at the same time enjoying the new power and status his brother's death conferred on him. Ernest would not have wished it this way.

The mourners climbed into their wagons, traps, and carriages for the ride back to the Crevetti winery, where they would all be fed and wined. Peter noticed the sheriff was present at the funeral. At first he thought the man was going to continue his unpleasant attitude of the evening before, when he all but directly accused Peter and Ernest of having strung up the two city agents, but instead the lawman went out of his way to pay respect to the dead brother's memory; they had gotten along none too well while Henry was alive, but that was now forgotten. The sheriff offered his condolences to Peter and accepted an invitation to the winery after the funeral. Peter had already spoken with Ernest and offered to back him every way he could so Ernest could take up where Henry had left off.

Throughout the ceremony, their mother clung to her youngest son, Tom. He had been the first of the brothers to be shot in this terrible trouble, but God had spared him. She was convinced it was her prayers that had saved him. Her oldest boy, Henry, had been beyond the power of her prayers.

When they arrived at the winery, the family's concern that all the mourners be properly taken care of helped distract them from their loss. Folks had journeyed from all over to pay their respects, and people met people they hadn't seen in years. Those not on speaking terms nodded stiffly to each other and avoided any confrontation that might be taken as a mark of disrespect to the Crevettis.

The weather was still mild, and so the feast was set up out of doors. Long wood tables were loaded down with food, and people were served in waves on Italian specialties as good as any found in the old country—a lot of people said—and the best reds and whites in the cellars.

"Goddamn brandy ain't fit for human drinking!" Raider scowled in his glass before taking a big swallow. "Least it's better than wine. What's wrong with people out here they don't drink whiskey?"

"Raider, maybe we should circulate and get to meet some of the Prospect ranch squatters we haven't come across yet," Doc suggested.

Raider helped himself to more brandy and thought about

it. Doc wandered away and got to talking with the younger men he figured might be active in any troubles. He let them know right off he was a Pinkerton, in case there was any misunderstanding. They seemed more relaxed and curious than anything else. He heard a lot of talk but nothing of consequence.

One man told him, "They been growing these here eucalyptus trees in the dry hills. I hear claims some of 'em grow fifteen feet in a single year. Brought 'em from Australia, where their timber is valuable. But you grow the same tree here and the wood shatters easily. No good as timber."

Another man told him about a forty-niner named Hugh Glenn. "Man was a college-educated doctor with a degree, but he never bothered with it. Never bothered to look for gold neither. He spent his time growing wheat in the Sacramento Valley. At the end of fifteen years, he owned fifty thousand acres and had made more money than the most successful gold miner. You just can't say what will work out best in the long term or where a man will finally end."

There was talk of the Silverado mine and the quicksilver mines at Redington. Any mention of southern California was enough to rouse a scornful laugh. And any story about a stupid Easterner down there was a real knee-slapper. Such as the fly-by-night operator who bought a tract of desert and stuck ripe oranges on the spines of the cactuses that grew there. He then sold high-priced lots to newly arrived dumb Easterners as producing orange groves.

Enrico Crevetti, who had looked like a gaunt scarecrow earlier on, was livened now by wine and company. When he heard Doc compliment a vintage and say he was surprised how difficult it was to find California wine elsewhere in America, he had an explanation ready.

"Last year I took an English gentleman on a tour of some vineyards. He made much the same observation as you, Doc. He hadn't even known we made wine in California till he arrived in San Francisco. He was so pleasantly surprised by the wine, he came here to see the Napa for himself.

The workers at the vineyard close to here that I took him to visit were labeling bottles when we arrived. The English gentleman looked at one batch and then at another. My neighbor grew a bit embarrassed, as he had a right to be, since the labels for his local wine all read Château this and Château that in France. The Englishman gave us a pleasant smile and said, 'Now I know why I've never seen a California wine elsewhere in America."

Doc's good intentions about meeting a cross section of the squatters on Prospect ranch evaporated when he met Vittoria Crevetti. She was one of the beautiful women the menfolk had made certain he was kept away from when he had dinner at the winery for the first time. Doc had seen her occasionally since that day but had never had an opportunity to talk with her before this. He figured he must be accepted by the family now, since no one interrupted them while they stood and chatted.

The day had grown quite warm, and Doc led Vittoria to the shade of an ornamental tree a little apart from the main gathering. She told him that she was a cousin of the family, a Crevetti in her own right, who had married a distant cousin, another Crevetti. The marriage had not worked out, and Doc understood from her hints that her husband had done something illegal or that had annoyed the family, and he had taken off. She now lived with an elderly aunt down the valley near Rutherford, not knowing for sure anymore whether her husband was dead or alive.

"He's been gone four years last month," she told Doc. "It probably doesn't bother him none not keeping in touch. I suspect he might even enjoy keeping me on tenterhooks as to what he's up to. He could marry again in some new place and no one would be the wiser. I can't do the same around here. A year back I was mighty tempted to invent a story—claim I'd heard he was dead somewhere so I could marry an auctioneer down in Oakville, but I knew soon as I walked out of the church door on that auctioneer's arm, first person I'd see at the bottom of the church steps, with a sneer on his face, would be my dead husband newly risen and come to haunt me. I realized I'd have no peace of mind if I went through with my plan, that I'd expect to see him at all sorts of odd times. My auctioneer married a pretty little Irish girl two months ago. He was a good catch."

Doc rose and helped her to her feet, and they set out on a leisurely walk along a grove of pines and oaks. Her body moved gracefully beneath her dress, which was in the latest simple fashion that Doc liked, not swollen with bustles and underskirts. Though Vittoria did not bare much skin, she knew a trick or two about how to reveal her body by the way she walked. She had smoldering brown-black eyes, long jet black hair, a narrow face with a vixen expression, and the kind of body a man would kill to possess for his enjoyment.

They picked their way through the pines and oaks on a twisting path.

Doc put his arm about her waist, and she snuggled close to him. After a short distance he stopped, took her in his arms, and kissed her gently on the lips. She made no attempt to resist, and the next time he stopped and held her again she returned his kisses passionately. They walked slowly along the path, halting frequently to embrace each other.

Doc took her breasts into his hands. He felt them surge beneath his fingers as he applied firm pressure, and her body trembled and she leaned against him with her thigh. Doc felt his erection grow, and the head of his cock, on its journey to the vertical, stroked her provocative thigh. His fingers kneaded her breasts and teased her nipples through the fabric of her dress, and she pressed her mound against his fully erect penis. He nibbled the skin of her neck beneath her left ear and breathed in the mixture of her natural body smell and her musky perfume.

Her fingers undid the buttons of his pants and ventured through the opening of his longjohns. Doc felt his true self spring out into the afternoon air, like a caged lion breaking through the bars. She enclosed his cock gently with her hands and then began to soft-stroke it and massage it, expertly exciting him further.

While he thrust his tongue deeply in her mouth, his right hand pulled up her dress, crept beneath it, and caressed the soft smooth skin of her thigh. His hand moved upward along her leg and then across a bare buttock.

"Stick it in me, Doc! Now!" Vittoria gasped.

His left hand reached beneath her dress and cupped the other buttock. Standing in the path, in the shade of the pines and oaks, he lifted her up by her shapely ass and felt her legs grip him around the waist.

He lowered her until the head of his cock felt the hairs of her muff, and he allowed his member to find its way into the moist aperture, which was already palpitating in welcoming rhythm. He hesitated a moment with only the head of his prick buried inside her, and then he allowed the weight of her body to impale her on the full length of his rigid shaft.

Vittoria moaned and tightened her legs around his waist.

Doc resumed his afternoon stroll along the path, and the jerking locomotion of his progress made the woman writhe and shudder in ecstasy.

While he sat on a fallen tree trunk, clutching her straddled on his lap, she went about satisfying herself, with much energy and rhythm, up and down on his ramrod. She cried out, and her body vibrated in a series of climaxes.

She lay against him, satisfied and exhausted, unmoving except for her slow, deep breathing and the rise and fall of her breasts.

Doc stroked and caressed her, kissed her, and ran his tongue over her neck and into her ears, and soon Vittoria was showing active interest in making love to him again.

Doc lifted her, still in place on his rock-hard penis, gently set her down on the soft leaves beneath the trees, and allowed the sword of the master to sink to the hilt within her.

CHAPTER EIGHT

Harry Jones was relieved to see all four men show up. He had paid them that morning in Napa City in gold, and it was Harry's experience that when you paid a man in gold, that was the last you saw of him. These drifters had to figure on easy money in a fat land to keep them from moving on. Harry had an idea that maybe they wouldn't earn their gold so easily from now on, but he wasn't telling them that.

"You boys are going to have some fun the next few days," Harry said to them. "I guarantee it." He ordered a round of drinks, though he could see that all four of them had more than enough already. "All I want you to do is keep putting the pressure on. On the railroad, on the squatters in general, and on the Crevettis in particular. You're going to find me visiting you up-valley from now on. I won't be sitting on my butt back in San Francisco while you boys do all the work—me and my brother are going to be right in this thing with you."

"Sure you are," one of the drifters said skeptically.

All four were smart enough to know that no man would

hire them to do a job he was willing to do himself.

"This train you'll be on going up-valley will be stopped north of St. Helena," Harry said. "I trust you'll give those boys any assistance they need."

"How come those dumb assholes always stop the train about the same place?" a drifter asked.

"On my orders," Harry said. "I want that train stopped on the Prospect ranch. Nowhere else."

"What about the sheriff? Why don't he poke his nose in?"

"He sympathizes with the squatters in an underhanded way," Harry answered. "He's a local man like they are. So there you have it. Both sides think robbing trains is helping their cause. Except I want to do much more than rob trains. I want you to force that sheriff into taking action—but make sure it's against them and not you or me. I'm going to leave things to your imagination."

None of them said anything, but at least they weren't complaining. Harry knew that with men like these, he had to convince them he wasn't putting one over on them. Being back-stabbing double-dealers themselves, they just naturally assumed he was one too. Which he was, of course, as he would readily admit anytime, but that was beside the point.

"That's my brother's land and my land," Harry told them. "A special act of Congress was passed just for us to get it. Now all my brother and I have to do is take it. But that's the problem. Congress says it's ours, but they ain't sending out the Army or U.S. marshals to help us possess it. We got to do that ourselves. And no California politicians or law-enforcement officers will touch us with a ten-foot pole because there's so many people squatting there on that big ranch. You gotta feel sorry for us—just two brothers against all them roughnecks and desperadoes. But justice will prevail. Mark my words, boys. You're on the side of the righteous."

They looked at him like he was crazy—or thought them crazy. But they said nothing. They gave a man a lot of leeway to run off at the mouth when he paid them in gold and paid them well.

Harry saw the four of them onto the evening up-valley train from Napa City station. He wanted to make sure they got on.

Each of the four men slumped into a double seat, stretching his legs out so no one could share it with him. They had spent their time since morning drinking, gambling, and whoring. With winter coming on, Napa City was filling up with miners down from the hills. A lot of miners liked to winter in the town and had nothing much to do after the season's work but amuse themselves. The town got real lively through the winter months, and the four men liked it so much they thought they might stay awhile. Since they'd been riding together, about a year now, they'd often talked about staying in one place for a spell—but then something would happen of a sudden and they would have to move out fast.

Past Yountville they felt rested and grew feisty again. One shot out a small glass wall lamp, and its fragments scattered onto the bald head of a passenger sitting beneath it. They had a big laugh at the man patting blood from his head with a handkerchief.

"Nice-lookin' well-to-do folks in this car," one drifter commented. "Let's see what they got in their pockets and purses."

They drew their guns and pulled their bandannas over their noses, although the people in the car had already seen their faces. Two men went to the front of the car, two to the back.

"Throw out yer valuables in the aisle if you know what's good fer you!" one bellowed above the rattle of the train. He repeated himself in case anyone missed the significance of his words.

Then the drifter with him reached across and pulled an earring out of a nearby woman's ear. She screamed in pain. He stood over her till she removed her second earring herself, then her rings, bracelets, and a brooch. The gunslinger kept the barrel of his Colt an inch or so from the nose of the woman's escort. This man threw gold and silver coins and greenbacks into the aisle.

The other three drifters hadn't moved, but their eyes flicked back and forth as they searched for trouble. Watches, necklaces, rings, coins, and bills were being dumped unwillingly in the aisle.

A taciturn man a couple of seats down from the woman who had lost her earrings did not budge. He caught the gunman's eye.

"You squatters ain't going to help your cause out on the Prospect ranch by robbing and harming those who have been giving you support," the man said firmly to the gunman. "Up till now you squatters ain't bothered us passengers, and we've put up with the inconvenience—until recently—of being able to go no farther than St. Helena because of your blockades. You think this is the way to show your gratitude?"

The drifter said nothing. He just holstered his gun and pointed to the floor of the aisle. The man shook his head, meaning he wasn't going to put his valuables there. The reluctant man looked like a farmer—he was heavyset, beefy, not used to being pushed about. The drifter was at least twenty pounds lighter, more sparsely built, but with muscles and sinews of whipcord.

In lightning-fast moves, he caught the farmer by the collar of his coat and heaved him to his feet, ducked a swing the farmer took at him, and kicked the farmer's left ankle, knocking both his feet from beneath him. The farmer fell heavily on his backside between two bench seats. The drifter caught him on the forehead with the heel of his riding boot, and the farmer's eyes rolled up in his head.

The drifter ripped open the pockets of the farmer's coat and pants, tearing away long strips of cloth, carelessly tossing valuables into the aisle and not bothering to retrieve anything that rolled under the seats.

He gave the unconscious man a parting boot in the ribs

and moved on to the next seats. The men sitting there turned their pockets inside out unasked in order to assure him they had parted with everything.

By the time the train slowed for Oakville, the drifters were ready to move to another car.

"No one gets on or off this car till the end of the line," one shouted to the passengers. "Anyone who gets off, we shoot."

They stayed on the train and directed passengers away from the car. The conductor grew curious, so they made him come with them to the middle of the three passenger coaches on this train, after forcing him to give the engineer the go-ahead.

From where he sat in the middle car, Willie McPhee saw the conductor enter the car at gunpoint. Neither Willie nor the passengers had any idea what had taken place on the passenger car immediately behind them. Willie knew that Paul Heron in the car ahead would in all likelihood not know what was happening here. Willie himself would have to stop these four men who were threatening the conductor. He looked for an opportunity to do so without endangering the conductor's life or the lives of the passengers. He was out of luck.

The drifter poked his boot in the railroad man's back, propelling his toward the open door of the fast-moving train. The conductor obediently descended the steps but balked at jumping out. The drifter reached for his gun.

Willie stood, shouted, and went for his weapon. The drifter spun around to face Willie, more than halfway down the car, without interrupting the smooth movement with which he drew his gun. He squeezed the trigger before Willie had managed to get his own gun clear of its holster. Willie felt a violent blow in his right shoulder, strong enough to knock him to the floor, and then he felt a slow flood of pain surge through his body.

"My God, I've been shot!" he gasped and saw the seats, windows, and interior of the coach recede and wobble in his vision.

The drifter turned his smoking gun on the conductor, who was still teetering at the open door of the speeding train, tightly gripping the brass rails on either side so the rush of air wouldn't suck him out. The railroad man, paralyzed by indecision, cast alternate looks of terror at the gunman behind him and the hard earth flying by beneath him.

The gunslinger smiled a satisfied smile at the conductor's terror, savoring it and increasing the man's fear further by goading him with his weapon. The fear-stricken railroad man, like a small animal trapped beyond hope of escape, made uncertain little fluttering moves and stayed where he was, incapable of action.

The gunman fired once, hitting the conductor in the back—the door now an empty rectangle of sunlight.

They had no trouble persuading the passengers of this car to put all their valuables in the aisle, along with their weapons.

Paul Heron had been surprised that the passengers getting on at Rutherford all seemed to head for the first coach. He hadn't been curious enough to investigate, being comfortable and bored in his window seat. In fact he had just been congratulating himself on the wisdom of his move to California. His wife and kids would love it here.

As the train pulled out of Rutherford station, a little late owing to the lack of the conductor's signal, Paul noticed four rough-looking individuals at the front of the car. They had taken a bottle of brandy from a luggage rack and were now passing it among themselves. They pulled their bandannas over their noses and continued swigging beneath them from the neck of the bottle. One cursed at the owner of the bottle, and when the man stood and tried to snatch it from them, he was kicked in the stomach and knocked back into his seat, where he remained doubled over in pain.

Paul had peaceably handled a hundred incidents worse than this. Just some drunk cowhands who meant no real harm. He approached them along the aisle with quiet dignity and authority. "Gentlemen, I will have to ask you to be seated and to moderate your language. If you do not, you will have to leave this train at the next stop."

He diplomatically failed to mention the bottle and the victim of its theft, which he considered a reasonable peace offering.

"Look at the fat freak," one drifter said and giggled.

Paul showed the man his railroad security officer's star and warned, "I meant what I said about the next stop."

The drifter, in very good mood, offered him a swig from the brandy bottle.

"No, thank you."

The expression in the drifter's eyes above the bandanna changed from one of devil-may-care tolerance to one of cunning viciousness. "You refuse my offer of a drink? Am I not good enough for you? You want to insult me?"

"Nothing personal about it, I just don't want a drink," Paul said firmly. "Now please sit down."

The drifter pulled a twelve-inch bowie. "What if I don't?"

Paul looked from one to the other of the four men. The three watched their companion in amusement. The knife wielder looked at Paul's big belly with interest—Paul had lost fifteen pounds since coming out west, but he had another fifty to go before looking trim and athletic again.

"You got a lot of wind, mister," the man with the bowie said. "I'm gonna let some out."

He darted the big bowie forward so that the tip of its blade penetrated Paul's vest and shirt and went a quarter inch into the layer of blubber beneath his skin. Paul yelped with pain, and the four men laughed.

"Hush, now," the man with the knife said. "Listen to hear if the air's escaping. Maybe the hole's not big enough."

Paul saw he was about to be attacked again and so he went for his gun. As his hand closed around the wood handle to pull the Colt from the leather, the bowie's blade came down in a sharp chop on the top of his wrist, opening a groove in the flesh that filled with blood.

Paul still clung to the gun and drew it upward. The blade

edge descended again, this time across the back of his hand. For an instant the white bones were visible before blood welled into the cut. The Colt dropped to the floor.

Paul defiantly faced his tormentor. He refused to nurse his wounds, and his right hand hung by his side. The blood ran down his fingers and dropped on the floor, splashing on his boots.

The man with the blade took the railroad security man's star from Paul's left hand and pinned it on Paul's chest.

"Take your hat off," he ordered.

Paul did so.

"Folks," the drifter yelled down the car. "You see here the security man of the Napa Valley Railroad Company passing his hat for your donations to a worthy cause. Anyone who don't want to contribute is free to discuss the matter with my three friends here."

He jabbed Paul with the bowie blade in his ample posterior to get him started.

Raider and Doc Weatherbee were talking with Tom Crevetti outside the family winery when a small boy rode up on a mule and shouted, "Mr. Tom, they've stopped the train again. They're loading goods."

Tom gave the boy a silver dollar, and he rode off in triumph.

"Where are you going, Raider?" Tom called after the big Pinkerton, who was already departing for the stables.

Raider turned and rasped, "Where the hell do you think?" He slapped the big Remington on his hip and set off again.

"If it won't inconvenience you too much," Doc called after him, "you might bring me my horse too."

Raider growled something that they didn't hear clearly, except that it involved something that Doc could do with his horse.

"Is he going to start shooting them up again?" Tom asked, alarmed.

"Only if they give him trouble," Doc said, none too concerned.

"Goddamn it, Doc, he shot me without good cause in the same situation."

"Only in the leg."

"I'm coming too," Tom said. "Make him wait for me, Doc. Those people aren't all real bad. Greedy, maybe. But only a few of them are real troublemakers."

"We'll see," Doc answered with icy coldness.

Tom Crevetti hurried to the stables for a mount.

Raider walked out shortly after, leading their two horses. When he saw Doc twirling the chambers of his Diamondback .38, he said, "So you've brought a gun! I thought you might be going to use a rolled-up newspaper today."

Doc said quietly, "Some people can achieve more with a rolled newspaper than others with a cudgel."

Raider flushed and changed the subject. "What's Tom all steamed up about? He was looking at me like I was a grizzly bear in that stable."

"He's worried about you shooting his neighbors."

"Why would he think I'd do that?" Raider asked, puzzled.

"Remember? You shot Tom, too."

"Oh, yeah. I'd forgotten that," Raider said sincerely. "You think that's been on his mind?"

Doc laughed and swung into the saddle. They waited for Tom, and all three rode at a fast pace down a side road to the stretch where the train was stopped most often. The sun was beginning to sink behind the mountains, which cast long shadows across the valley floor.

As they neared the railroad line but still could see nothing through the trees, they heard the locomotive work up steam and chuff in the direction of Calistoga.

"I thought you had arranged for them to wait for you after any incident," Tom said.

"There's a doctor in Calistoga," Doc said.

Tom said nothing to that, and they listened to the train heading away up-valley. Next they heard the cries of men driving horses and the creaking of wagon wheels on the road ahead. They met five wagons, each pulled by four horses, with two men aboard each big load and seven out-riders. Three against seventeen. The crates and casks on the wagons were marked TO THE SILVERADO MINE, NAPA COUNTY, CALIFORNIA.

The men greeted Tom Crevetti guardedly but kept a hostile silence with Raider and Doc as they halted the wagons.

"Bring 'em right about," Raider bellowed. "We're taking this stuff back where you got it from."

No one budged or said anything, waiting for someone else to make the first move. Only Raider wasn't waiting. He drove his own horse against the lead pair on the first wagon and forced them to move in a wide turn back the way they had come. The horses of the second wagon began to follow of their own accord. Then those of the third.

A bullet snapped away a fragment of the collar of Raider's leather jacket. Raider twisted around to the right in his saddle, hauling his Remington from its holster as part of the movement. His thumb was already pulling back on the hammer before his eyes located the telltale wisp of smoke from a carbine carried by one of the mounted squatters. The man was pumping another cartridge into its firing chamber. Raider's dark and deadly eye lined up the shot in an instant, and his gun hand and trigger finger, working as one with his brain and eye, guided the instrument of destruction.

The .44 lead projectile left the barrel with a tail of flame like a comet and split apart the forehead of the horseman with the carbine. As a blow struck to a weed's seedpod scatters its contents, Raider's bullet emptied this man's skull of all thought of killing him. For a moment he remained rigid in the saddle, eyes staring vacantly ahead and bloody matter streaming down his face. Then he crumpled, rolled off the horse, and lay in a disjointed heap on the earth.

Raider looked calmly around at the other squatters on their horses and on the wagons. Their faces were gray with shock, and their eyes furtively traced Raider's gun in fear of their lives. Raider beamed at them benevolently and eased the big Remington back into its leather.

He said, by way of kindly advice, "With me, you gotta make your first bullet count."

It was nearly dusk by the time the wagons reached the railroad line. Tom Crevetti rode with the squatters, talking with them. Doc and Raider rode behind, Raider ready with his carbine to pick off anyone who might try leaving suddenly. No one did. Not after a look back at Raider, and not after remembering the accuracy of Raider's last pistol shot.

Tom recognized the squatter Raider had killed as a troublemaker named Cale, who had brought a bad name on the others. They told him that the train conductor had been killed and Willie McPhee wounded by four hired guns sent by the Jones brothers. McPhee had been hit in the right shoulder but not badly—he was weak from loss of blood more than anything. So they thought. The four men had badly beaten Paul Heron, but Heron had recovered enough to look after McPhee. Heron had ordered the train on to Calistoga to bring McPhee to the surgeon there. The four hired guns had ridden away on horses, no one knew where.

They had reached the rails by the time Tom had finished his account of this to the two Pinkertons. Doc said nothing. When Raider heard that Willie had been shot, he cursed and swore up a storm and threatened to kill every man jack of the squatters there. He rode up and down before them in the failing light, as they waited and wondered what they should do, fearing their least action might set this loco Pinkerton off on a killing rampage.

"I don't believe no fucking four hired guns!" Raider roared. "You little shit-faced yellow bellies shot that man, and you're going to pay for it. I want the man who shot him! You hear? The rest of you can go. Just give me the man who shot him. I'll give him a deal. Fair and square. Fastest to slap leather walks away. I can't offer anyone a fairer deal than that."

When none of the squatters stepped forward, Raider pulled one man off a wagon by the scruff of the neck and beat him around the ears. The man whined like a cur.

"Who did it?" Raider bellowed into his ear from an inch away.

"Th-the four—"

"I don't want to hear that shit!" Raider shook him, and the man whined like a whipped dog again. "Point him out to me!"

The man blubbered something unintelligible, and Raider let him fall to the grass in disgust.

Tom said, "Leave him alone, Raider, before he dies of fright."

"You feel sorry for this worm, do you?" Raider came back at him. "Did this worm feel sorry for a wounded Pinkerton lying in his own blood on the train while he was stealing stuff from the boxcars?"

Tom had no answer to that.

Raider wheeled his horse about. "You still got your weapons, shitheads. I left them with you. So you could draw on me. Go ahead. Any or all of you. Try it."

Raider went on some more, but the squatters stuck to their story that four hired guns had done the shooting. Raider tied a noose in a lariat and threatened to lynch one man. Tom tried to defend the squatters, while Doc stayed well back—as Raider knew he would—his Diamondback .38 concealed but at the ready in case the squatters took Raider at his word and tried to gun him down. Finally Raider had to give up because of approaching darkness. He collected their weapons in a burlap sack and tied this to his saddle pommel.

"You louses wait here till that train comes back and load these stolen goods back in the boxcars where you found them. I don't care if you have to wait till this time tomorrow night. I want all of you—not some of you, *all* of you—to wait here till you put that stuff back." He turned to Doc and Tom. "Let's go."

Doc walked closer to the group of disarmed squatters so he could see their faces more clearly in the dusk. In contrast to Raider's hellfire delivery, he asked in a subdued voice, "Which you brought the four horses here for the hired guns?"

No man said anything, but several gave involunatry glances at one man.

Tom said, "That's Carver, a friend of Cale, the man you just shot, Raider. I think maybe both of them have been working for the Joneses all along. They manipulated the rest of the men here, like they manipulated me at one time."

Doc said politely to the squatter, "Mr. Carver, I think you should ride with us and have a talk."

The man went to his horse.

"Well, I'll be darned," Tom said admiringly. "After all that hootin' 'n' hollerin' you was doing, Raider, which brought you nothing, good old Doc hooks a live one for himself while hardly speaking in a whisper."

Raider gave Tom a dirty look and spat. "Night ain't over yet."

Doc Weatherbee tried sweet-talking Carver, Raider threatened him with mutilation, Tom Crevetti advised him as a friend and neighbor—all to no avail. Carver would admit nothing.

"We got you on robbing a train," Doc said firmly. "You were caught red-handed. Should be good for six or seven years in jail if we turn you in."

"No judge or jury is going to find me and all the others guilty of that in this county," Carver said with a calculating smile.

"All what others?" Doc asked, looking puzzled.

Carver replied. "The other sixteen men who were with me tonight—fifteen counting the living."

"I saw you and Cale with the stolen goods," Doc said. "Cale's gone. That leaves you. You see anyone else, Raider?"

"Carver and Cale, that's all."

"You're in a bind, Carver," Tom said. "You've been offered the chance to go free no matter what you've done if you cooperate. You're a fool to turn the chance down."

"Better do time in jail for robbing than take a bullet in the gut from one of Jones's men for talking out of turn," Carver said decidedly.

"All you'll have to do," Tom said persuadingly, "is lie low for a while until these Pinkertons here wipe the Joneses off the face of California."

Carver had a laugh at that one. "Harry Jones would have these two for breakfast."

"End of conversation," Doc murmured.

They were all hungry and tired. It was already late, and Carver looked as if he could hold out against them all night. The lamps cast a yellowish glow over the three men sitting on barrels in the upper floor of the winery. The oak barrels, imported from Europe because the wood from American oak species gave too strong a flavor to wine, lay on their sides in four long rows. Each had a bunged hole in the top. From time to time Tom had them sample various aging wines, from the previous year's vintage to one five years old. They made Carver stand while they sat, and refused to let him drink or smoke. Yet he still looked as if he could outlast them.

Raider impatiently walked through one of the stone archways that led from the second story of the winery onto the flat roof where the grapes were crushed. Thousands of stars burned brightly in the clear sky above his head. The air was mild and fresh. He was sick and tired of looking at Carver's cunning face. Carver thought him stupid. Carver was afraid of Doc, respected him. Raider decided it was time he took action.

When Raider returned to the interior of the winery, he said to Tom and Doc, "Why don't you go over to the kitchen of the house and have something to eat now. I'll watch this varmint, and you can bring something back for me. Then we'll all head into Calistoga tonight, stick this joker in the town jail, and go see how Willie is doing."

After Doc and Tom had left, Raider lay back on a barrel, head and shoulders against the wall. He shuffled about until he was comfortable, then closed his eyes. Carver watched him warily, presuming a trick. Dog-tired from standing so long and being harassed, Carver sat on a barrel himself. If Raider was only pretending to doze, he would fly into a rage and make him stand again. Carver figured that sitting on a barrel wasn't quite enough to get him shot by Raider.

When Raider slumbered on, Carver began to reckon his chances of getting Raider's six-gun from its holster. He decided he might be able to get the gun, but would almost certainly wake Raider and have to shoot him, thus alerting the others without giving him a head start. He would be even worse off then than he was now. No, his best way was simply to tiptoe out of here, vanish, disappear into the night. If things went well, he'd look into the stable for a horse. At first light he'd collect some belongings from home and head up into the hills for a week till things blew over.

Carver rose and stealthily made his way across the floor to the stone arch, and from there out onto the flat roof. The stars shone above, and he gratefully breathed in the night air. Freedom was at hand!

Then he heard a sound behind him. He looked back and saw Raider's outline silhouetted by lamplight in the stone arch. He heard the Pinkerton shout a curse. Carver decided against jumping the fifteen feet or so from the flat roof down to the ground in the darkness in case he sprained an ankle. He chose to run the length of the roof to where it merged into the hill.

A bullet whistled past him, and he heard the roar of the gun. Then another. He zigzagged and ran as fast as he cold along the roof. Then he felt his feet give way beneath him, his body hit a sharp concrete lip, he felt himself falling, dropping down, sinking into a heavy clinging liquid that surged above his head, deep, deep. . . .

Carver swam to the top of this strong-smelling pond, things sticking to his face and hands. He looked about him in total darkness. A round circle directly above his head revealed stars. He swam some feet to one side and came against a smooth wall into no handholds. He would have to keep swimming or sink. It was only by the smell that

Carver knew he had fallen into a vat of fermenting grape juice and skins.

Raider went back inside the winery to fetch a lantern. When he had been out on the roof previously, he had opened all the trapdoors into which the grape-crushing machines fitted. Now he didn't want to fall into one of his own traps. He went around closing the trapdoors methodically and in no particular hurry until a voice inside one called up to him.

"Help me. I'm here."

Raider set down the lamp and gazed down by its light at the man swimming in the sticky mess beneath. He chuckled. "Better not piss in their wine, Carver, or you'll make the Crevettis mad."

"Pull me out, Raider. I'd do the same for you."

"Like hell you would. My advice to you is take it easy, 'cause you're gonna have to swim all night till someone gets here in the morning. Might be another week before they find your body in here if you sink."

"All right, Pinkerton. You got me. I'll cooperate."

"Suppose I fished you out and you changed your mind. I'd be mad enough to shoot you."

"Get a rope! I can't last much longer!"

"You going to testify in court against the Jones brothers?"

"Yes! Anything! My arms are giving out!"

Raider had a length of rope already coiled around his waist. He dropped one end down to the struggling man. Shaking his head, Raider said, "That's the trouble with me, I'm all heart. I just can't say no to anyone who needs my help."

Harry Jones peered out the second-floor window to see who was banging on the door of the farmhouse at this hour of the night. He could see the outline of the horse and rider by starlight, but he couldn't make out who it was. Harry made no sound, lit no light, gripped his Colt Peacemaker and watched through the grimy pane.

"It's Bingham, Mr. Jones. Open up. I have news for you."

Bingham, the lawyer from St. Helena, had rented this house for him so he could get closer to the Prospect ranch yet remain undetected and safe from his enemies there.

Harry lit a candle, stumped down the stairs in his night-shirt, and opened the door.

"Bingham, I told you to stay away from here. If you're going to beat a trail here to see me about every legal quibble that enters your mind—"

"This is important, Mr. Jones. The Pinkertons have killed Cale and put Carver in the care of the town marshal of Calistoga. He's to be taken to Napa City courthouse to-morrow to lay charges against you."

Harry paused to take this in. "How do you know all this?"

"As you know, I work two days a week in Calistoga. I was there this evening when they brought him in, looking like a drowned rat. He was completely covered in sticky red guck he got from falling in a wine vat. My guess is the Pinkertons tortured him. I went immediately to the jail and tried to bail him out. Carver refused and said he didn't want to see me. I told the marshal that this sounded mighty peculiar and I had difficulty in believing it. He was locking up for the night and told me I could find out for myself by going round the back of the building—Carver was in the cell of the southwest corner with a barred glassless window at ground level. The security precautions are laughable at some of these small-town jails. I persuaded him to talk with me. He said he was afraid you'd have him killed if I bailed him out because he knows too much and could be dangerous to you. I told him he was talking nonsense, but by the time I had talked him around to accepting bail, the marshal was gone. Carver then told me how he was trading evidence against you in exchange for the Pinkertons' dropping train robbery charges against him. I went to the marshal's house— but he's a cantankerous independent-minded man who's not got much use for me personally. In spite of a generous private offer I made to him, he told me I'd have to wait till morning to bail Carver out. However, those Pinkertons will probably be there too, and they won't be willing to part with their prize witness. I thought that if you came with me back to Calistoga tonight and both of us saw the marshal, we could free Carver—"

"Go home, Bingham. Be sure people see you back in St. Helena tonight. I'm a righteous, upstanding man. That brigand's testimony can't harm me."

Bingham looked at him like he was raving. Then he saw the sly grin on Harry's face and knew he had best be gone.

Harry waited until the lawyer had found his way out of the dark deserted farmyard on his horse before going back inside the house. Harry knew he could depend on the lawyer so far as paperwork went, but when it came to muscular rather than legal action, lawyers were notoriously weak-kneed. If they couldn't fix thing in ink within a clause or plead it in ringing tones before a judge, they were of little use.

He lit a cigar and took his time in getting dressed. No doubt Bingham would be fussily careful about picking his way on horseback in the dark, and Harry wanted him well out of the way before he left the house himself. It was almost an hour before he departed, allowing the animal to search its own way in the dark.

His horse's hooves thudded softly in the dust on the main street of Calistoga. This place was no hell-raising cattle town. Come nine at night, nothing much moved but owls and coyotes. The jailhouse, Harry knew, was set off from the other buildings. He found it easily by starlight and hitched his horse nearby.

The barred window of the southwest cell had a broad stone sill at Harry's chest level. A prisoner could buy food, alcohol, or even sex through these bars after the marshal had gone home. Harry could see nothing inside.

"Carver!" he hissed.

He had to call repeatedly before a low voice told him to go away. Carver had heard all along and hadn't answered. Such lack of respect angered Harry, but he kept his temper in check.

"I've decided to pay your bail and give you $150 an acre for your land if you and your family skip town right away."

"You'd do that?" Carver asked uncertainly.

"It ain't because I'm feeling generous. This is the cheapest way out for me."

"Be a lot cheaper for you to have me shot," Carver said.

"Wouldn't cost me a nickel," Harry agreed. "But it's too risky right now in case something goes wrong and the blame is traced back to me. I could lose millions in trying to save thousands. So spending a few thousand on you is a good investment. And we might do business together someday further down the line. Things happen that way."

Carver came to the barred window. "What do I do?"

"Let Bingham bail you out first thing tomorrow. He'll give you some money to live on in hiding while he draws up the land agreement. After a few days you contact Bingham, and when you sign the agreement he'll hand you your money. You contact him when and where you like. Bingham ain't going to gun you down."

Carver laughed at the thought of the clerklike lawyer even knowing how to use a gun. "Sounds reasonable. I'll do it."

"You stink, Carver. You been drinking?"

"No, I fell in a vat of fermenting red wine. My clothes are stiff as boards. The stuff has dried to my skin—if a fly landed on me, it would stick. Tell Bingham to bring me fresh clothes."

Jones laughed. "That's what I smell? You're covered with half-fermented juice? I don't believe it."

"Touch my shoulder here and feel for yourself."

Both of Harry's hands stretched in between a pair of bars. In a rapid movement, whose sleight of hand would not have shamed a magician, Harry looped a braided rawhide thong around Carver's neck, thrust his knee against the wall of the building, and pulled mightily outward on the ends of the braided thong with his gloved hands.

It was not a clean job. Carver's position was responsible for that. Had he had his back to Harry, the rawhide thong would have cut off his windpipe totally and he would have died with a struggle but fairly quickly.

As it was, Carver had thrust his left shoulder to the bars for Harry to feel, so he had been caught sideways. As the thong squeezed tightly around his neck, each time Carver managed to wrench about to partially face his attacker he found relief, because the thong's pressure eased on his windpipe and was taken instead by the spine. Harry had to twist him around as well as keep up the pressure on the thong so his head could not slip out and escape. If that happened, he would then be beyond reach in the cell. A disaster!

Carver weakened from the struggle, and in the end Harry managed to hold both ends of the thong in his right hand and push Carver about with his left. Still the squatter died noisily, croaking and gurgling like a pondful of frogs—but it was nothing that would wake the town.

As Harry walked back to his horse, he took off his gloves. They were sticky and had a winy smell.

Harry smiled and said to himself, "Goddang! That son of a bitch really was in a wine vat."

CHAPTER NINE

"Stow that shit," one of the four said. "We don't care about your crap legal rights to this land. If you want to stay in with the Joneses and not get evicted, number one, you'll feed us, and number two, you'll tell us what's been happening the past few days. We been living up in that chaparral in the hills. Thorns there enough to cut a man and his horse to pieces. What's that on the stove?"

"Stew."

The drifter looked the farmer over. The farmer began to feel that maybe he was being a bit unfriendly, considering the circumstances—which was a surprise visit by four dust-covered, unshaven horsemen to his solitary farmhouse, where only he, his wife, and his two boys lived.

"Feed us." It was an order.

The farmer fetched four bowls and made to ladle stew into them.

"My friend, that's woman's work, as I see it," the drifter told him. "Tell your wife to serve us. I say food always needs a woman's touch."

"She's in town with my children," the farmer said. "Gone

to Calistoga to buy cloth to cut into clothes."

The drifter nodded to one of his three companions. The man walked past the farmer, up the stairs that led from the kitchen to the story above. When the farmer made as if to stop him, two of the drifters whipped out their revolvers and snapped back the hammers. The farmer froze in mid-step. There was the sound of a sharp cry and a woman's footsteps on the stairs. With a firm grasp of her forearm, the gunslinger pulled her with him down into the kitchen. When a boy about nine forced himself between them, the man struck him with his other hand and knocked him down. Again the farmer stepped forward, and again two revolvers stopped him.

"Feed them, Winnie," the farmer told his wife.

Her hands trembled as she ladled the stew into the bowls. She spilled some on the stove top and on the front of her prairie dress. She was a plain, big-boned woman, used to working out of doors and with no time for nonsense. She was a simple woman, and her strongest emotion now was fear for her family and herself, which her trembling hands gave away. Her boy picked himself up and sat on one of the lower stairs. His younger brother, maybe five, watched things from the top step.

The men ate greedily, slurping the stew from spoons. They emptied the pot on their third helping.

"You got any whiskey?" one asked.

"No," the farmer said.

"Brandy? Wine?"

The wife spoke up. "This is a God-fearing house. I don't permit the demon rum under my roof. Right here in this valley, the devil's plant is spreading. God's rich grassland is being uprooted, and the tree of evil is spreading its vines and tendrils everywhere. Not for nothing, mark you, it its fruit called the grapes of wrath."

"Amen, sister," one drifter said. He turned to the farmer. "We met someone on our way down from the hills who told us you and your friends talked to the Pinkertons about us."

The man glanced nervously at his wife before replying. "They caught us with the stuff off the train and tried to blame us for killing the conductor and shooting the other Pinkerton. We weren't going to take the blame for that."

"So you turned on us," the drifter snarled.

"It wasn't just me," the farmer said. "They be saying you wore bandannas over your faces on the train so people would think you were squatters and blame us for everything. We got enough troubles of our own without you coming here to stir up more for us."

"You got troubles all right," the drifter said in a menacing tone. He winked at the others. Then he patted his belly and said to the farmer, "A gutful of warm food gets a man to thinking of other comforts. You tell your woman here to come upstairs with me."

"Never!" his wife screamed.

Up to this the farmer had let them intimidate him, but now he jutted out his jaw at them. "Git outta here! We got no time for your kind in these parts. You go tell those two Mr. Joneses they can't tread on us. I want you out of my house, off of my land. Now!"

They didn't move and hardly paid attention to him. They were looking at the woman.

The one who had suggested she go upstairs with him walked across the kitchen to her. "You gonna walk up them steps ladylike, or do I have to drag you up them?"

"Get away from me, you filthy devil!" she screamed.

He slapped her face and grabbed her hair. With his hand twisted firmly in her long hair, he bowed down her head and pulled her screaming toward the staircase.

The farmer charged at him, teeth bared and eyes wild with rage. The kitchen resounded with a shot, and they all heard the stifled moan of the farmer as he sank to his knees, clutching his side.

The one pulling the woman behind him kicked the nine-year-old off the stair.

* * *

Doc changed the dressing on Willie McPhee's shoulder wound. "He did a good job on you; there's no infection. You had the same surgeon that fixed Tom Crevetti's leg after Raider shot him. Tom had no bad effects, and your wound is looking just as clean as his did. You've been lucky, Willie. There aren't that many medical men out west with skills like this surgeon has."

"I'm feeling fine," Willie said. "My right shoulder is a bit tender. Otherwise I'm fit as a fiddle. You see my new gunbelt?"

Doc had. It was not a new belt—it was new only in the sense that Willie had borrowed it from one of the Crevettis and that it had a left-hand holster.

"I can go back on the job now," Willie said happily.

"Don't fool yourself," Doc told him. "We're putting you on a train back to Chicago. You rest there for a month and you'll be right as rain."

Willie looked at Raider in appeal, in the reasonable belief that he would disagree with anything that Doc said. Not this time.

"You ain't fit, Willie," Raider said. "You could get yourself or someone else killed by not being able to handle the job. You gotta be the judge of that yourself."

"That's what I'm doing—I judge myself fit," Willie said impatiently. He took his right arm out of the sling. "See, I can move it with no trouble, reload with it, keep my balance, everything. I only use the sling to support the arm in order to rest my shoulder. And I can shoot nearly as good with my left hand as my right." When this statement was met by a disbelieving silence, he said, "Come outside. I'll show you."

Raider and Doc took him up on that, and Willie was pleased, knowing that he had more than half persuaded them already to let him stay on. They walked out of the Crevetti winery into one of the vineyards, and Willie looked about for something on which to demonstrate his marksmanship. There was nothing much except the straight lines of vines and their big leaves. He spotted some bunches of late-ripening grapes hanging in one line of vines. He quick-drew with his left hand and chopped up the clusters of soft fruit with .45 slugs. Then he used his right hand to reload quickly, and he again temptied the six chambers on more grape bunches.

Raider was impressed. "I wish I had a left hand!"

"All right, Willie," Doc said. "You can stay."

Tom Crevetti came out to investigate what the shooting was about. He broke off the clusters of damaged grapes. "You're lucky my father didn't see you do this. He'd have gone for his shotgun and used it on you. I bet he misses these bunches. I think he knows every plant individually on this land."

"All the more reason he should keep it," Doc said.

When Paul Heron rode in from Calistoga, Doc looked at the stitches on the wounds on his right hand and belly. Paul was pleased to hear Willie would be back with him on the train. While the others were occupied, Paul slipped Doc the latest telegram from Chicago.

Mistake to see railroad trouble in terms of larger conflict. Essential that operatives restrict themselves to duties assigned, except in the most exceptional circumstances.

Wagner

"The clerk handed it to me just like that," Paul said. "I had read it before I realized it was for you, not me. What are you going to do?"

"Wagner is playing smart. He's not directly ordering us to ignore the land conflict regardless of consequences. If he did that and things worsened, we could blame him. I suppose my reports may have put him in a difficult position." He tore up the telegram and smiled when he saw the look of surprise on Paul's face. "Don't mention the telegram to Willie. I don't want to disillusion him about Chicago by seeming to ignore their orders."

"I never thought I'd see you tear up orders from headquarters, Doc," Paul said.

"It's all a matter of interpretation. Wagner knows exactly the game I'm playing with him. Look out for Willie on the train. I think you two should ride in the same coach while he's still hurting."

Heron and McPhee left for Calistoga to catch the down-valley train. Tom, Doc, and Raider rested themselves in the shade of a tree. Almost all the grapes were fermenting in the vats, and the harvest was nearly complete. A sense of completion and well-being now reigned at the winery in place of the frantic activity Doc and Raider had seen when they first arrived. But all three men knew this was a false security. As it happened, it lasted somewhat less than an hour, broken by the arrival of the farmer's nine-year-old son and a neighbor on a buggy. The boy was incoherent.

The neighbor talked out of earshot of the boy. "I picked him up on the road a couple of miles from their farmhouse. It seems the four desperadoes who killed the conductor on the train shot his father and raped his mother. They might still be there if you ride hard."

"Take the boy to our house," Tom said. "They'll look after him. Doc, Raider, I'll show you the way."

They got to the farm at a fast clip. At the house, the woman sat on a kitchen chair by the prone body of her husband. He was dead. Her five-year-old sat on her lap, sobbing. She was beyond tears, her dress torn, one eye almost swollen closed, her lower lip split and bloody.

Tom said, "Your boy is safe at our home. We'll hitch up a wagon for you now. Both of you go there to stay the night. We'll look after things here."

She nodded gratefully.

Doc talked gently with her while Tom readied the wagon. Raider scouted about the farm till he picked up the tracks of four horsemen leading off into the hills. He couldn't follow them far because of the dry ground.

After the woman and her child had departed in the wagon, the three men were divided on what course of action to take. They covered the body, and Tom said he would arrange for the funeral next day. They finally agreed to visit farms in the area to ask if anyone had seen or knew anything.

Some men were friendly and brought them into their homes. Others were willing enough to talk but kept the Pinkertons out of their farmhouses.

"Maybe we might have seen some missing railroad property," Doc said. "I hope they realize that we have more important concerns than that."

Tom remembered a brother of the woman who had been attacked. He didn't live on the Prospect ranch but right next to it.

After the man got over his anger and sorrow at the news, he told them, "I can't help you myself, but I know those who can."

He saddled a horse, and they followed him to a falling-down cabin in the foothills. Children played about in front of it, and at the sound of their horses a woman came to the door, drying her hands on her apron. She didn't have to tell them where her husband was—and maybe she wouldn't have—but at that moment the sound of ax blows came down the hill. They nodded to her and rode up the hill through thorn bushes. The man stopped his work and looked them over as they approached, leaning on the handle of his ax.

"Those four blackguards who paid you to buy them food, tobacco, and whiskey have raped my sister and killed her husband. I'm guessing you could tell me where to find them."

The man with the ax shook his head. "I delivered the goods to them at the crossroads below. I don't know where they went after that."

"You're a lying scum! You know my sister. They hurt her! I know you well enough to bet all I have you followed them. If a man were to offer you fifty dollars, he'd find you know more than you now pretend."

The man tested the ax-blade edge with his thumb. "I think you might be right."

Raider put in, "No one's paying you money, scum."

"Then no one finds out what they want to know."

Raider dismounted and unbuckled his gunbelt. He dropped

the weapon and ambled unhurriedly toward the man with the ax. The man hesitated a moment, then decided he could hold off this big dude, though he was a little worried by the confident way he dropped his shooter and figured to take on a man and ax with his bare hands.

Raider gave him another chance. "It's not as if we're trying to take something off you that don't belong to us. You're hiding murderers from us, and in my eyes that makes you one of 'em too."

"Cost you fifty dollars," the man said, wielding the ax before him in both hands.

"I'll ram that ax handle up your ass before I pay you a nickel," Raider ground out.

"Twenty dollars."

Raider only laughed.

He reached for the shaft of the ax and missed. The man chopped at him with the steel head, and Raider had to throw his body to one side to avoid the blow. He regained his balance fast and came at him again. Swinging the ax rapidly from side to side to keep Raider at bay, the man backed off.

"Ten dollars," he offered.

Raider laughed and lunged again. This time he got under the ax as it was raised to strike him. As the blade descended, he grasped the shaft with one hand and stopped it in midblow. He twisted the ax handle sharply to the side, breaking the man's grip on it, while he bumped against him, knocking him off balance.

Raider now had the ax. With a loud whoop, he raised it over his head and took a wild swing at his adversary. The man avoided the blow only by falling on his back as the slashing wedge of sharp steel whistled over his prone form.

Then Raider stood directly above him and brought the blade down in a fierce swipe directly at the man's face. The man screamed in terror and jerked his head out of the way. The cold steel of the ax blade buried itself in the earth inches away from his left ear.

"Log cabin," he gasped. "Cabin out past Henderson Hollow. Left there by the miners. I followed them there. They didn't see me."

"I don't believe this asshole," Raider growled and pressed the ax handle across the man's throat.

"I swear... I swear.... Tom Crevetti there, he knows the place."

The man wheezed desperately for air till Raider released the pressure on the shaft across his throat.

Raider said, "You dumb bastard. You protect men who made one woman a widow. Your own wife could've been next. If we don't get them, I hope they come here and kill you. And if they don't come, maybe I will."

The winery was not far out of their way, and they went along with Tom's suggestion to pick up his brothers Peter and Ernest. From the winery, the five men rode beyond the boundary of the Prospect ranch. They passed a deserted house.

"That's not the place," Tom said. "The log cabin's a couple of miles farther on."

Harry Jones trained binoculars on them from a window of the empty house. He thought for a moment they were coming for him. When they passed the house, he guessed they were after the four gunslingers he had found a place for down the trail. Harry reckoned they could take care of themselves and the best thing he could do was look out for himself. It was almost certain that someone at some time had seen him coming or going, and it would just be a matter of time before the Pinkertons came to check this house also. His four hired guns would sell him out too if they had anything to gain by it. He would let the Pinkertons and the Crevettis go on a piece, then saddle up and ride out....

Doc looked at the log cabin with disapproval. The ground had been cleared for hundreds of yards all around it.

"Not much in the way of cover," he said.

"There's no way for them to sneak out, either," Raider said.

"We got only one way to go. Ride right up in the open

as if we were going to pass by. Then attack suddenly."

Neither Raider nor any of the Crevetti brothers looked as if they thought much of this plan. However, since all five were already out in the open area, they had not much choice but to ride on. Doc eased his way out in front, one hand searching in a saddlebag. He brought out two sticks of dynamite laced together with a fuse.

"I collected these from the wagon when we stopped at the winery," Doc said.

"I don't smoke," Raider said to Tom. "Got a match?"

When they were exactly opposite the log cabin and as near as they could get to it without raising suspicion, Doc shouted, "Come out of there or we come in and get you."

There was still no sign of life from the cabin. Raider knew it would have been safer for them just to attack without warning, but he remembered how he and Doc once had a gang of bank robbers trapped in a tumbledown shack. Or so they thought. Doc insisted on shouting a warning, and six young children emerged. The bank robbers had tricked them and were long gone.

"Ain't no kids here, Doc," Raider said. "If they want to shoot it out with us from behind those logs, they might as well be in an Army fort."

The glass of one of the cabin windows broke and a rifle barrel poked out. Raider struck the match, touched the fuse, and Doc threw the paired sticks. They turned end over end in an arc and landed at the base of the cabin's front wall.

The door flew open and a man ran out to pick up the dynamite and throw it back before it exploded. A rifle cracked. The man staggered and fell. Peter Crevetti pumped another shell into the chamber of his smoking rifle.

The second man out the cabin door took the full force of the explosion. He was lifted high into the air and seemed to float there a moment above the flash before he slumped down in a lifeless heap.

The front wall of the cabin collapsed into a jumble of rolling logs. Dust and smoke mingled in the rubble, making it impossible to see.

The Pinkertons and the Crevettis had been washed by the shock wave and blasted with small stones and dust. It took them all their strength to control their mounts.

"Let's go!" Ernest Crevetti yelled and charged forward on his horse.

Doc and Raider shouted after him to hold back, but their success at killing two of the drifters so easily had gone to Ernest's head. His younger brother Peter had got one with his rifle. Now it was his turn.

He galloped right up to the collapsed wall of logs, over which the pall of dust and smoke still hung. A single shot came from inside the cabin. The horse wheeled about and ran back toward them, with Ernest clutching his chest but managing to stay in the saddle. His two brothers and Doc helped him off the horse. Doc saw he was badly wounded and sent Tom back for a wagon. While they tended Ernest, Raider took on the drifter who had fired the shot from the cabin. Whether the fourth drifter was there too, Raider had no way of knowing. There was no sign of horses nearby, and he guessed they were tied in a clearing in the woods in order to leave the impression the cabin was still deserted. Raider rode his horse as near to the cabin as he judged wise, keeping as much of the animal's head and neck as he could between him and the cabin. Grabbing his carbine, he dismounted swiftly on the far side of his horse next to a close-up stump of a tree. It was the best cover he could find on the cleared ground about the cabin. He whacked his horse on the flank, and it trotted off.

Raider lay on the ground behind the meager cover the short tree stump offered. The collapsed logs of the shattered front wall of the cabin provided a barrier about four feet high. The cabin roof and the other three walls remained intact, and the interior was almost dark. Raider's eyes scanned the one-room building for movement. He waited.

He saw nothing until a gunflash revealed the position of a rifle. The rifleman was standing directly behind the tumbled logs and resting his weapon on top of them.

The first bullet kicked up dirt a few inches to one side

of the tree stump. The second hit the stump and ricocheted almost straight up into the air in front of Raider's face.

Raider gauged where the rifleman stood behind the logs and triggered four bullets into the crack between two logs at the level of the man's gut. He couldn't be sure he got him, but at least the rifle quieted down. Raider ran to the side of the cabin. Two revolver shots rang out, but both bullets were way wide of the mark—although Raider was a big man and presented a bigger target area, he was fast on his feet and very difficult to hit when moving.

Putting down his carbine and drawing his Remington for its faster shooting capability than the lever-action gun, Raider peered around the edge of the wall into the cabin interior. A body lay on the wood floor with several bloody holes in the midriff. One hand still clutched the stock of a rifle. This was the rifleman he had managed to kill through the space in the logs. The fourth drifter was inside somewhere, his revolver ready.

Raider carefully edged around some more from behind the side wall in order to have a better view inside the cabin. The last of the drifters caught him by surprise as he did so, appearing from beneath some of the fallen logs directly in front of Raider. He had caught the Pinkerton off balance and open to a clean pistol shot. Raider knew he would be too late with his Remington, so he flung himself sideways against the fallen logs. He caught the end of one log with a thrust from his shoulder. The log gave way, and its other end swung about and hit the gun arm of the drifter. The blow sent the drifter's shot at Raider wide. But it didn't knock the weapon from his hand.

The drifter raised the Colt at Raider's head as he sprawled helplessly among the logs. Nothing could save Raider now— too late for him to use his own gun, too late to throw his bowie. Unless the drifter's gun misfired—and Colts didn't often do this. The drifter was enjoying his situation. Raider saw his thin-lipped smile as he was about to press the trigger. . . .

The drifter spun about and fell lifeless on his side, the

Colt held loosely in his hand. The shot was so timely and the marksmanship so precise—a shot to the head—that Raider didn't have to look to know who had fired it. He felt relief, but also irritation. Any old shot would have done the job—there was no need for Weatherbee's persnickety goddamn perfection at a time like this.

They got Ernest home, and he lived on for a few hours. He never regained consciousness and died in bed with his family gathered around him.

Raider spoke with Doc privately after the death. "We gotta stop these amateurs from interferin'. They don't know what they're doing and get killed like bugs on glass."

"You're having one of your guilt attacks, Raider. It's not your fault anyone has gotten killed, let alone Ernest. If it weren't for you, a lot more decent people might have died. So don't blame yourself. The Crevettis are fighting for their land. We can't stop them from fighting any more than we can stop the Jones brothers."

The family took the second brother's death hard. The mother wailed and leaned on Tom. Old Enrico was rock steady but looked smaller, more shriveled and wizened than he had before. The worst moment came at the graveyard while Ernest's coffin was being lowered into the gaping hole in the earth, next to the fresh mound of earth that covered Henry's body. Peter began to curse and rant. He swore he would kill, he would have vengeance. . . . The priest looked up from his prayer book but could not quiet him. Raider and Doc led Peter away so the graveside prayers could continue.

Tod Jones's stocky figure had become familiar to San Franciscans as he made campaign speeches at street corners around the city, bought beers for the house in taverns, greeted families leaving churches, everywhere promising everything to everybody. Now the final push of the campaign was under way, and his workers continued to detect a general lack of enthusiasm on the part of the populace for Tod Jones as

U.S. senator. Some of the campaign workers said Tod had to make even more speeches and bigger promises. Other workers said the public had already seen too much of him and he was better off lying low for a while. Tod opted for more speeches and not only promises—this time he would give the voters *guarantees* they would get whatever they wanted if they sent him to Washington.

Harry Jones was staying in the background as much as possible and taking all the responsibility for the happenings on the Prospect ranch up in the Napa Valley. Tod's opponent had made what Tod called vicious unfounded allegations against him on the land dispute and had quoted the Crevettis as saying he was responsible for the death of their oldest son. Now that another Crevetti son had died, according to the newspapers, Tod would have to expect fresh attacks from the same source. He had no choice now but to keep away from all this completely and leave it for better or worse in Harry's hands. All he could do was hope it would be over as soon as possible. With the Crevettis evicted or dead, the bankers would unroll their red carpets for him and perhaps round up some important votes in the business community as well.

The morning's activities went well. After a substantial lunch, Tod arrived for a short speech on Market Street. He was becoming practiced at saying a few high-sounding words and then making a round of smiling handshakes. He even enjoyed it.

One of his listeners in the Market Street crowd disturbed him, a strange individual with a heavy ginger mustache and thick reddish hair several shades darker than his mustache. He met the man's eye several times as he spoke to the crowd—it was almost as if Tod couldn't avoid doing so, such a baleful unwavering stare at him.

Speech finished, Tod smiled his smile and shook hands all around. He thrust his hand out to the red-haired stranger, who still stared him in the face. The stranger's hand came out—to meet his handshake, Tod thought, till he saw that it held a miniature pistol. Tod even noted the make—a five-shot .22 Remington Elliot, the one with the ring as a trigger, with a curved trigger stop behind it. Tod owned one himself.

The man with the ginger mustache and strange red hair pumped three little bullets into Tod and managed to escape in the general confusion after the senatorial candidate fell.

CHAPTER TEN

The assassination of the aspiring politician Tod Jones by an unknown hand was greeted with jubilation on the Prospect ranch. "Pity Harry wasn't there too," was a sentiment expressed by many. Others theorized that Harry had in fact been responsible for his brother's murder so that he would get everything. In spite of rumors that railroad attorneys were on urgent business in Washington, no one in the Napa believed any longer that a peaceful solution could be found for the squatters' problem. Thus they saw Tod's death as the removal of part of the problem. Harry's demise would be a big help too, according to general opinion.

Harry Jones made statements to the newspapers accusing the Prospect ranch squatters of complicity in his brother's murder. Reporters claimed that the surviving Mr. Jones kept armed guards about him twenty-four hours a day, which he promptly denied. The *Napa Reporter* and *Napa Register* and small-town newspapers carried this big-city news, and Harry's innuendos that the Crevetti family was behind his brother's assassin were regarded as ludicrous. Valley people controlled things in the valley. They were considered rubes in the city. People laughed at them in the city because they had never learned its slick ways—and never would, they hoped. Although a man could go to San Francisco, do what he had to do there, and be back in the Napa in a single day—a round trip of a hundred miles by road, rail, and water, such were the wonders of modern transportation— in reality San Francisco was as distant as the moon to most hardworking, simple valley folk. The idea that some of them might have gone in to that noisy metropolis of bargaining and sin to kill a candidate for the U.S. Senate was beyond the scope of their imaginings.

Things were happening in the Crevetti family that had not been foreseen. Old Enrico had gone in on himself after the deaths of his two oldest sons. The once loquacious patrician of the family now hardly spoke a word to anyone. He seemed either unaware or uncaring of what went on around him. He rarely even entered the winery anymore and had been seen on his walks to pass damaged and sickly vines without apparently noticing them.

His wife leaned more than even on her youngest son. However, those who had previously called Tom a mamma's boy, claiming he lacked the backbone of his three older brothers, noticed a new man emerge as responsibility bore down more heavily on him.

After the oldest son's death, the family leadership had been picked up without question by Ernest, the next oldest. Now that Ernest was dead too, Peter was next in line. At first it seemed that this transition of power would take place as smoothly as those before—until Ernest's coffin was lowered in the grave and Peter interrupted the priest's prayers with his curses. From that moment on, Peter showed no interest in small everyday events on which decisions had to be made, decisions which were a great deal less than earth-shattering but nonetheless essential to the family's well-being.

"Ask my brother," Peter would snap at people when they came to him with minor problems.

So people started to come to Tom without first consulting Peter, wishing to avoid his ill humor. Peter would talk only in terms of Family Honor, of Vengeance, of Retribution, of Victory. Such things make fine talk, the country people said, but they don't cure a sick hog.

Willie McPhee spent some days laid low with a fever, a kind of delayed response to the shock of being shot. He still refused to admit he had pressed himself too hard and had been on his feet again too soon after his injury. The fever had hardly passed before he was back on the trains again with Paul Heron.

Paul was regaining his optimism about California. It had been shaken by a poke and two chops of a bowie blade. He had learned some new things about himself—that he no longer really wanted a life of action, that he was perfectly content to pass his days filled with security and peace on this little train riding up and down the fertile valley. He looked forward to the time when he could spend his evenings with his wife and children in their own home in the valley. Also, he had lost another seven pounds.

Doc and Raider were less accepting of appearances, but shared their opinions only among themselves.

"If someone had gone after Harry to kill him," Raider said, "you could easily believe it was over some private quarrel that had nothing to do with the Prospect ranch. He's got a crowd of enemies. But when Tod, the churchgoer and baby-kisser, who everybody feels sorry for because of his terrible twin brother, when he gets shot, it's hard to believe it wasn't someone from here in the Napa, where folks know what Tod is really made of."

"I'm forced to agree with you," Doc said.

"Don't put that in any of your reports or we'll be hauled out of here like hooked fish."

"I already have," Doc said. "Along with the relevant newspaper clippings."

"Asshole."

* * *

Raider always removed himself from the house to leave the coast clear for Doc Weatherbee and Mrs. Jackson toward the middle of the day. Unknown to Raider, the widow Jackson could always tell by his continued presence that Doc was not coming to see her that day. At such times Raider always denied he knew Doc's whereabouts, which of course only added to Mrs. Jackson's suspicions and jealousy.

It irked Raider enough that Doc should have such a never-ending supply of devoted women, but it drove him plain crazy that this widow female gave him nasty looks over Doc's unexplained absences which she never dared give to Doc himself, the one who cause her doldrums.

"Where is he?"

"I dunno."

"Of course you do!" she would say petulantly. "Stop protecting him!"

"Lady, our Pinkerton work is confidential. You got questions, telegraph our Chicago office."

"You're such a boor!"

Either Raider would ignore her at this point in the conversation—all these conversations between them were remarkably similar—or he would stalk out in a bad mood, saddle up, and gallop off to more peaceful surroundings. There was no staying in his room during the day, because the Chinese women made it impossible with their cleaning, chatter, and curiosity.

Raider was constantly on the point of leaving for a hotel in Calistoga. But good home cooking, convenience, and the easygoing atmosphere (when Doc was around) always made him change his mind at the last minute. All would go well till Doc disappeared again.

"Where is he?"

"I dunno."

And so on.

Of course Raider did know. Doc was down near Rutherford with Vittoria Crevetti, whose elderly aunt took the train to Calistoga several days a week for "treatments" at the hot springs. Vittoria stayed home for her "treatments." Doc usually returned on the evening train, resplendent as a peacock. "Resplendent" was a word Raider learned from Mrs. Jackson, a word which became firmly associated in his mind with burnt food and glowering sulks.

Raider was therefore completely surprised on the occasion the widow pecked him on the cheek, in Doc's absence, and told him he was cute. He was horny as hell, and before he had properly considered what he was doing, he had run his hand up her dress along the inside of her leg. She screamed like a stuck pig, and about a dozen Chinese women ran into the room and started to hit him with table ornaments, pieces of paper, their fingers, and other deadly objects. He tried to explain, but it only made them more hysterical.

After that he decided it wasn't safe for him to be in the house alone with them, outnumbered as he was.

Harry Jones owned everything. Tod's widow and children settled for the lump sum he offered them rather than live on in hopes they would one day come into possession of the Prospect ranch. In the widow's view, the ranch had caused the death of her husband, and she wanted nothing more to do with it. Harry was glad to relieve her of this burden. The papers were signed. Everything was his.

None of the niceties and hypocracies so essential to politics could hold him back now from claiming what was his. Harry was running for no public office, and never intended to ask anyone for a vote as long as he lived. He had no need of the good opinion of others, either now or in the future. They were welcome to think what they liked of him, and so long as their thoughts didn't interfere with his plans and transactions, more power to them.

Harry had heard the rumors that the Napa Valley Railroad company lawyers were in Washington to discuss the act that granted him and his late brother the ranch land. Officers of the company admitted to him that they had sent lawyers to the capital on a confidential, unrelated affair and denied that it concerned the Prospect ranch. Harry didn't believe a word of it. He knew the saying that possession is nine-tenths of the law. It was more urgent now than ever before that he come into rapid possession of the Prospect ranch.

As he walked along the streets of San Francisco, Harry was conscious of the inquisitive looks directed at him by passers-by who recognized him. He was glad they could see he was not afraid to walk alone wherever he pleased—without the armed guards the newspapers claimed he had. In Harry's view, if he couldn't strike fear into those who opposed him, he was finished anyway and might as well be six feet under. His coat was tailored to conceal the big Colt .45 Peacemaker he always carried.

He stopped to look at a new street of houses under construction. The street climbed a sharp hill, and the carpenters were setting the floors of the new houses at an angle to the incline to keep them level, so that the uphill side of the house was even with the ground and the downhill side elevated four or five feet. There were hills with even greater inclines than this in the city, and Harry knew they would all be built over with houses as land grew scarcer and more expensive. They had laughed at Tod and him when they first arrived from the East and bought hillside properties. The locals thought they were duping greenhorns. Instead it was their own lack of vision that caused them to sell cheap. Harry didn't own this particular hillside on which the street was being constructed, but it warmed his heart just to look at first-rate houses going up on land that previously had been regarded, because of its steep incline, as fit only for cabins and shanties.

Cheered by the thought of future profits from his hillside properties, the hammering of the carpenters music to his ears, Harry stepped lightly on his way. He greeted those he considered more wealthy or powerful than himself and ignored those less so. In all cases the men he greeted responded to him warily rather than in a friendly manner, but they responded. Harry Jones was too dangerous for any man to snub.

He walked along in the noontime bustle of this mild f

day, with winter rain threatening and a strong smell of the sea in the wind. Gulls screamed over the housetops.

His mind swung back to the Prospect ranch. This land loomed in his mind in an increasingly powerful and obsessive way. Even if he had wanted to cast thoughts of the ranch from his mind—and he didn't—he would not have been able to. This land would make him rich beyond anything he knew now. All that stood between him and this great wealth were the grinning, malevolent devils squatting on what was now legally his.

He entered a waterfront chophouse, turned down the manager's offer to guide him to a select table, and walked through the crowded premises, scanning the faces. His gaze finally settled on a stout, plainly dressed woman in middle age with a booze-reddened face. He approached the table and removed his hat.

"Ella?"

She pointed to the empty chair at her table. "I was about to give up on you."

"I was unavoidably delayed," he lied.

"Our kind gets jittery waiting about."

"Ah, I didn't know you had . . . difficulties in this state."

"Two of us have," she said in her flat voice. "Goes back ways, but there's them who never forget."

Harry was not easy to impress, yet there was something solid and menacing about this woman that left a lasting impression on him. Her gray eyes were as friendly as slivers of slate. Harry assumed that the rough-looking type at an adjoining table, who was using his hands to stuff food into his chomping mouth, was one of her associates—presumably one of the Greenaway Boys who was not wanted by the law in California.

Harry ordered mutton chops for Ella and himself, red wine to go with the food, and another straight triple gin for the lady.

Vittoria Crevetti met Doc Weatherbee at Rutherford station. On the short train journey down, Doc had taken the opportunity to chat with Willie McPhee and Paul Heron. Both men had been keeping a sharp eye out for anyone who looked as if he might be a hired gun sent to the valley by Harry Jones.

"Been very quiet, Doc," Paul said. "It's the time of year, with winter coming on. You have men coming in from the hills, not going up there. So we'd immediately notice any hardchaws traveling up-valley. There's been none so far we haven't been able to account for by asking a few questions behind their backs."

"Quiet before the storm," Doc warned.

Paul wondered whether it was too early yet to bring his family out west. He needed some time off to find a nice house. He smiled hopefully and said, "I suppose this isn't the right time yet for me to take off for a spell?" When Doc did not reply, Paul said disappointedly, "I thought not."

While Paul was distracted, Doc said quietly to Willie. "Now don't you go retiring to the soft life. Stay on edge, Willie."

Vittoria met Doc with a buggy drawn by an elderly horse and they moved at a stately pace along the tree-lined streets to the edge of town. As they drove along serenely, listening to the birdsong in the gardens and the hum of bees among the flowers, Doc looked forward to some hours between the perfumed sheets of her bed. The old aunt was dipping herself in the hot springs of Calistoga and wouldn't be back till late afternoon at the earliest. By then Vittoria and Doc were usually downstairs again in the parlor, having tea and conversation.

Doc glanced at her beside him on the bench seat of the buggy. She was looking at him with her vixen expression and her brown-black eyes smoldered. She brushed a strand of her long black hair from her face and sighed.

"Tom Crevetti wants me to marry him."

Doc was not as surprised by this news as Vittoria probably expected him to be. He had seen the controlled envy with which Tom had regarded him in Vittoria's presence. Doc was also pleased at her news but would not let her see

this, since she would presume from it that he was glad to
be rid of her. Which was not the case.

"Are you going to?" he asked.

"Depends."

Doc refused to be led into the question of what it might
depend upon. "Aren't you close relatives?"

"No, only second cousins."

"Remember when you told me about not marrying that
auctioneer in case your previous husband showed up again?"

"Tom brought the news that a body found in Wyoming
has been identified as his. That sets me free."

Her smile as she said this showed that her belief in Tom's
story was less than absolute.

Doc asked, "What if he does show up?"

She shrugged. "I guess Tom will take care of it."

"Don't call the Pinkertons."

She laughed and was silent for a while. Then she said,
"You didn't say what you think about my marrying Tom."

"I like him. Of all four brothers, I've found him the most
likable. I'm sure he knows about you and me."

"He does," she said matter-of-factly. "I told him I'd ask
your opinion before I said yes to him."

Doc wondered exactly what she meant by that. He assumed that if he said no to her marrying Tom, he would be
under an obligation to marry her himself.

"I think Tom and you will make a great pair," he said
with sudden enthusiasm.

"Then this afternoon is goodbye between us, Doc. I know
Tom would expect me to stop seeing you."

"That's reasonable," Doc conceded. "But I hope we don't
have to say our farewells here in this buggy."

"I don't think we should go back to the house, Doc."

So much for the perfumed sheets, Doc couldn't help
thinking. He was going to miss Vittoria in the days ahead.
At being suddenly deprived of her in the middle of the day
made this even worse.

The ancient horse tottered along a strange lane, so senile
it had lost his way home. They let him go where he willed.

"Remember the first time we made love?" she asked, putting her hand on his arm.

"I'll never forget it," Doc said, trying desperately to recall the event.

"We walked away from the crowd at the house after poor Henry's funeral and followed that little path through the trees...."

Doc remembered now. He put his arm around her and held her close to him.

Then he saw what had brought this to her mind. It was not a grove of oaks and pines, like the one they had walked in before, but the southern exposure of a hill covered with bushes that enclosed little grassy spaces. There was no physical resemblance between the two places, but Doc knew what she had in mind. He steered the horse onto a small meadow, where the animal stopped of its own accord and grazed. Doc jumped from the buggy and assisted Vittoria to the ground.

A distance into the shrubs, they came across a small clearing with thick grass, warmed by the sun. Without word, Vittoria daintily disrobed. She stepped naked and graceful across the clearing to a small tree, broke off the tip of a branch, and turned to face Doc with the green leaves protecting her modesty.

Doc stripped. He had to chase and catch her before he pulled her lithe body to his. He darted his tongue inside her mouth. She snuggled up to him and thrust her pelvis against his. Doc felt the excitement surge in his body. He cupped her firm, rounded ass in his hands. For a woman who did no physical work, she had an amazingly fit body.

He pulled her tightly against him and let her feel the pressure of his hard cock straining against her skin. Then they lay together on the grass, feeling and groping each other in lusty abandon.

Her body was as hard and supple as that of a dancer's. Vittoria showed little sign of passivity in her lovemaking, and while Doc was still caressing her breasts and stroking her legs and belly, she bent over his throbbing member and sucked it into her warm moist mouth.

In a little while, when Doc tried to roll her on her back in order to enter her, she resisted and murmured, "I want you this way. . . ."

They lay on the grass on their sides, face to face, and Doc felt her guide his penis into her slippery, juicy opening, and felt the head of his large cock seized by the muscles of her vagina as she permitted him to enter her only a half inch at a time while she rubbed and chafed her clit on his member.

Her body convulsed in a violent and prolonged orgasm before he had sunk the full length of his shaft in her belly, and she sobbed helplessly and hugged him close, so that her tears ran down his face as well as her own.

"Having to say goodbye to you is going to be the hardest thing of all for me to do," she whispered fiercely. "I just want you to know that. I'm not going to say anything more."

Doc felt the muscles of her vagina contract as she became aroused again. He thrust gently into her, and his cock pushed apart her tender inner lips. . . .

Peter Crevetti burned the red wig and ginger mustache after he shot Tod Jones. Everything had gone exactly as he had planned it. But it had been easy only because the attack was unexpected and the target very accessible. Killing Harry Jones would be another matter entirely. Harry would be expecting an assassin and would have made preparations. At first Peter feared that the surviving Jones brother would go into hiding, which he could quite easily have done, and direct his operations from some lonely, fortified ranch house. If Peter had understood Harry Jones better, he would have known that going into hiding would never have occurred to Harry, and that if someone had suggested such a thing to him he would have taken it as a deliberate insult.

Harry thrived in the midst of his enemies. He was known to say he preferred San Francisco to New York because in the much smaller western city he was bound to meet his few friends and his many enemies every day.

Peter Crevetti didn't understand the mind of a man who enjoyed seeing other men cringe before him more than he enjoyed shaking their hands as equals.

Jones's stocky body, with his barrel chest, broad shoulders, and oversized hands, was powerful. Whatever else he might be, Harry was no physical coward. Though at forty-six he was fifteen years older than Peter, they seemed to Peter to be of about equal strength, and Jones could probably make up what he lacked in speed and agility through cunning and experience as a city street fighter. But Peter had no hero's visions of an evenly matched contest to the death between the two of them. Peter knew that if he tried to fight fair, Jones would fight dirty—and win. Peter wanted only one thing: to murder him, pure and simple. As he had murdered Jones's brother. As Jones had murdered two of Peter's brothers.

Peter was no physical coward either. He knew the risks he was taking by coming into San Francisco after Harry Jones, bearding the lion in his den. He knew he was more likely to make dangerous errors in the city than he would in the more familiar territory of the Napa.

His first mistake was to take at face value the indifference of city people, to think he could wander the docks anonymously, just another face in the nameless thousands of faces. In fact everyone from the police to dockside thieves asked one another who he was and who or what he was waiting for. Somehow word got around he was a Russian sailor—perhaps because of us heavy black beard and the long black coat he wore—who spoke no English. Peter deliberately avoided saying a word to anyone lest they later claim in a court of law that they had spoken with him and could thereby recognize him. The Russian sailor was said to be strange in the head and best left alone because he was subject to fits of violence and was strong as an ox. Someone had seen a group of drunk sailors returning to their ship try to rob him; he beat two of them so seriously they were carried away, and he chased another one with a knife, who dropped his weapon and ran. It was only a matter of days before he was a well-known dockland character, and new arrivals to the port supposed the "mad Russian sailor" had been a fixture of the place for years. In spite of all this, Peter Crevetti fondly imagined he had blended in with his surroundings, unnoticed by all, indistinguishable from the rest.

His second mistake was not to kill Harry Jones the first chance he got. Peter knew him well to see, as he did Peter, from their court appearances in the earlier stages of the land dispute. But even if Peter had never set eyes on Harry before, he would have recognized him as a raffish, sporting version of Tod. Harry was leaving a restaurant in the company of two prosperous-looking men, the sidewalks were crowded, the streets congested with wagons and carts, Harry was arguing with the two men and oblivious of Peter's presence only a few steps away, Peter had the .22 Remington Elliot in his hand, a live shell lay in each of the five chambers . . . yet Peter did nothing.

Afterward Peter tried to explain it to himself. It had all seemed too easy. He had been in the city only a few hours, having prepared himself to spend days stalking his quarry before he found an opportune moment to strike. And here, almost immediately and without any special effort, the man he had come to kill unconcernedly provided him with a perfect opportunity. There was something in himself, Peter decided, that demanded opposition before he could act. Everything at that chance moment fitted in too well with his carefully laid plans—he would run around some corners in the crowded streets, pulling off his beard as he went, then his long black coat, and walk away as outwardly calm as he had done after killing Tod, but with his heart beating so loudly inside him he couldn't hear the city sounds about him.

Peter knew too late he would never get another opportunity like this to kill Harry Jones. He had let fortune slip through his fingers. He had sought opposition. Now he would find it.

His third mistake was in believing what Harry Jones told the newspapers. Of all people, Harry was the last Peter should have taken at his word. Although, in a way, Harry spoke the truth when he told reporters he didn't have men guarding him day and night. At the time he said it this was true, and it was during this time that Peter let slip his opportunity to slay him outside the restaurant. Harry told the newspapers that he was too proud to need gunmen to protect him on the streets of San Francisco, that he despised any man who let his fear rule him to that extent.

By now Peter had seen Harry, and Harry had seen the mad Russian sailor, several times a day, every day, day after day, in the dockside area. Peter's opportunity was never going to improve. He decided that next time he saw Harry, whatever the circumstances, he would kill him. There would be no more delays. No more second thoughts. No excuses. . . .

Harry came walking along a block of warehouses with that arrogant stride that particularly irritated Peter. He would kill him now, this time without fail. Peter would have preferred the docks more crowded. It was Sunday, and the schooners and brigs rode softly on the harbor's protected waters, each with only a two-man watch, starboard and larboard. The wharves were deserted except for a lone woman and a few old men sitting about, the kind of salty dogs who come down to watch the ships and who spring upon the unwary with long stories of rounding Cape Horn in foul weather, with royals and skysails fore and aft, and losing the main top-gallant mast.

Peter made no pretenses. He drew the miniature Elliot and rushed toward Harry Jones, determined to put a few of the .22 slugs in him at point-blank range to make certain they did the job. Jones saw the mad Russian sailor in his full black beard and long black coat charging him and reached for his Colt Peacemaker, knowing already that he was too late. . . .

As the bearded man ran past the lone woman—a plainly

dressed, stout woman with a coarse, reddened face—she drove the sharpened tip of her parasol at his side.

She managed only a glancing blow. It was more the shock and sudden pain of this unexpected attack that caused the bearded man to stumble and drop his little pistol than any disabling effect of the slight wound itself. He recovered immediately and was stooping to pick up his weapon when he was clouted behind the right ear with a short length of lead pipe the woman had handy in her purse.

"God bless you, Ella," Harry told her with sincere emotion and gratitude as he gazed down at the semiconscious insane Russian sailor at his feet.

Harry did not connect this attack to his troubles in the Napa Valley.

Harry lifted him by the armpits and Ella took the ankles. At the dock edge, they swung him back and forth and let go on the third heave. The black-clad bearded man hit the dirty harbor water with a splash.

The old men hobbled hurriedly away from the docks. The seamen on watch aboard the ships were too far away to interfere. Ella fetched her parasol and purse, then picked up the fallen .22 Elliot. She walked back to the edge of the dock, where Harry stood looking down into the water.

Peter's fourth mistake was not knowing how to swim. Sudden immersion in the chilly seawater had cleared his head. He now threshed about panicky in the deep water. At first the air trapped inside his long coat helped keep him afloat. Then the wool coat absorbed water, and the trapped air bubbled out through the top and front. The long sodden coat further weighed him down and restricted his movements.

Harry looked with interest and enjoyment at the spectacle of the drowning man. When Ella raised the .22 pistol to take a potshot at him in the water, Harry placed his hand on her wrist and smilingly shook his head.

Together they watched the insane Russian sailor wallow and splash till he sank out of sight. Only his hand reached out above the surface and clutched at the empty air. Then it too was gone.

Ella and Harry had already turned away when a false beard surfaced on the dark filthy water and bobbed on the little harbor swells.

CHAPTER ELEVEN

Like Doc and Raider, the Greenaway Boys had been too young to fight in the Civil War—but they remembered it well and had cause to do so. The war had brought death, separation, division, and loss of land to their families. They had been reared outside the small town of Greenaway, Missouri, not far from where the James brothers hailed. Jesse and Frank were their heroes.

They had come a long way since then. Five states and the Indiana and Montana territories. Murder, train and bank robbery, rustling, horse thieving. Bob, Clem, Zak, Joe, Walt. Joe and Walt were brothers; Ella was their sister. Zak was a neighbor to these three; Bob and Clem were their cousins. They had all known each other since childhood.

Rob the rich and feed the poor. Ella and the Greenaway Boys were known to have started out that way, and folks back in Missouri liked to remember them like that. Things had never been that way in reality—they sure as hell had robbed the rich all right, and they had given stuff they didn't need to cousins and friends. But they always found that when it came to robbing, they couldn't be too particular who they robbed, rich or poor. And when it came to feeding the poor, they found it hard to imagine six more deserving people than themselves.

The five men rode down from their hideout in the Napa range, east of the valley. They rode down the rocky, arid slopes with their covering of scrub oak, pea chaparral, mountain mahogany, manzanita, and buck brush. The prickly leaves and thorny branches scraped and cut them. They cursed.

"When's Ella coming here?" Zak asked.

"Hell, she ain't coming out here so long as she can sit tight in Frisco," Bob said.

"Now that ain't true," Ella's brother Walt put in. "We all know she roughs it with the best of us. So stop bad-mouthing her."

"That's right, Bob," Ella's other brother, Joe, added. "If she hears you been saying stuff behind her back, she'll kick your butt."

Bob laughed.

They sighted a small house in a grove of pear trees and rode up to it. Unwashed breakfast plates and coffee mugs lay on the table, but there was no one about. Zak emptied out two kerosene lamps over the walls, stood in the doorway, and tossed in a lighted match. As they rode away, none of them bothered to glance behind at the house in flames.

The next house wasn't far away; they could see it across some fenced-in grassland. They broke down the fences as they rode directly for the house.

Wrecking the fences turned out to be a mistake, since it forewarned the residents of the house that these newcomers were up to no good. The owner of the land loosed off a rifle shot over their heads before they even got close to the house. They veered away, smashed another fence, and found themselves on a small dirt road, which they followed west-ward, down into the valley.

As they went, they overturned a wagon, drove cattle onto

a vineyard, let horses loose, and burned another house after letting a woman and her three children escape from it.

No one crossed them, and they felt they were having fun this morning, so no one got hurt. The Greenaway Boys liked to claim they were never the ones to begin shooting. At one farmhouse they had a big lunch of sweet sausage and green peppers washed down by red wine. They felt so sleepy and good-natured after the meal, they didn't burn the place, as they had intended.

Their mood changed fast next place they came to. By this time word had spread that they were about and that they could be chased off if folks stood up to them. When they were seen heading for Foster's Creek, some kids on the watch-out galloped ahead to warn the first house down the road. Four of this man's neighbors had brought their weapons and their grown sons. They prepared to give Jones's five hired guns a hot reception.

Elsewhere on the Prospect ranch, vigilante groups were being formed to cut off the five men's advance farther into the valley.

"Jones has sent them here to burn us all out," was the common explanation.

The frequent answer was, "Even if he burns what I got, I'll stay on in a sod house or under canvas before he gets my land."

The man and his neighbors waited in ambush behind the trees on both sides of the road. When the five horsemen appeared a distance away, the men checked their weapons once again and pressed down into their hiding places.

It was all blown by one boy who couldn't stand the tension of waiting anymore. He fired his Winchester while the Greenaways were still a long shot down the road and brought down the lead rider's horse. The other horsemen wheeled about, and the downed rider leaped up behind one of the others. Then the four of them galloped away in a cloud of dust, untouched by the wild fusillade of of shots fired behind them.

They bore left on a road that was hardly more than a

pair of wagon ruts with grass growing high in the middle. A big frame house, painted green and yellow, stood behind a windbreak of pines.

"I need a horse," Bob called, stating the obvious.

They rode up to a corral near the house in which fresh animals came to greet their horses at the rail. Bob found a saddle nearby, caught an animal, and saddled it with Clem's help.

"Hey, what's going on there?" a man yelled from the front door of the house.

"Don't bother us," Clem shouted back.

A rifle bullet zipped off the corral rail next to him.

"Damn, I'm sick of people shooting at us and all we do is turn tail," Clem yelled. "Time we taught these clodbusters a lesson."

Clem left Bob with the horse and ran to his own to pull his rifle from its saddle sheath. He fired from the hip on the green-and-yellow house as he ran forward. No one fired back at him as he ran—there had been only one shot, and the man had disappeared inside the house again. The four others made no move, content to wait where they were and watch what Clem would do.

Clem stood outside the house. The door was open. The lower half of the ground-floor window to the left of the door was raised, and a pair of lace curtains billowed in and out in the breeze. Clem ignored the open door, walked to the window, and looked in. Then he put a match to one of the curtains, which disappeared in a sheet of flame.

By the time Clem had rejoined the others, blue smoke was pouring from the open window.

The man and his wife and children ran back and forth from an outside pump with buckets of water and threw them on the flames. Red and yellow tongues of fire now licked up the side of the frame house, and the blue smoke had turned to black. From where they were, the five horsemen could hear the crackle of the dry timber being consumed.

"Let's go," Bob said, anxious to try out his new mount.

"Hell, that bastard tried to kill me," Clem complained.

As the others moved off, Clem hung back. He waited till he saw the man hurrying with two buckets of water, raised his rifle, and dropped him with a single shot.

As Clem caught up to the others, he looked back and saw the woman and children bending over the man, who lay next to the two buckets fallen on their sides.

Raider sat at the bar in the Pair of Fives in Calistoga, having heard that some of the Greenaway Boys had showed there twice in the last few days. Raider knew how dry a man could get in a hideout up in the mountains, especially with armed bands of vigilantes waiting in the foothills. A few drinks in a nearby town could sound like a mighty great idea. Raider said nothing to Doc before he left. Showdowns in taverns weren't Weatherbee's style. And Raider didn't need to hear his considered opinions on the subject. Truth to tell, Doc was getting on his nerves more than ever, both of them stuck out in the Jackson woman's house.

He nursed his drinks slowly, knowing he might have to depend on his reflexes before too long. That half second that too much booze slows a man can cost him his life.

Several of the men at the bar had greeted Raider, which was a big change in their attitude toward him. His stock was rising as things grew worse—which was nothing new. They were forgetting now how he had cracked down on their robbing the trains, and they now saw him as a powerful ally against Harry Jones.

One man Raider recognized as a Prospect ranch squatter sidled up to him with an empty glass. Assuming that the man's only purpose was to touch him for a drink, Raider poured him a whiskey from his bottle.

The man spoke out of the side of his mouth. "Mind you, you didn't hear this from me, but I seen one of them fellas who been burnin' places go with Harriet. Leastways I think 's him."

"How sure are you?"

"I saw him riding with the others day before yesterday. s the same man."

.

Raider left money on the bar and slid off his stool.

"You know where Harriet's place is?" the squatter asked.

Raider grinned and nodded.

He walked down the side street to where her cabin stood on the edge of town. There wasn't much night life in Calistoga, and Harriet was its shining attraction. She was a nice person, too, and Raider was willing to go out of his way to make sure she wasn't hurt. This meant he would have to wait in the darkness till the man left alone, rather than burst into the cabin and take him by surprise, as he would have preferred to do.

A light shone in Harriet's curtained window. Raider found himself a comfortable spot beneath a big tree in which to wait unseen. He was soon feeling the chill of the night, and had to flex and unflex his fingers to keep them warm and fast-moving.

It seemed like two hours before the door of the cabin opened and cast a long sliver of lamplight on the dusty ground. A man laughed, and then his figure was silhouetted in the doorway for a moment as he put on his hat. He closed the door after him, which extinguished the glow of lamplight. Raider could see his shadowy form in the darkness. He knew the man's eyes would not yet have adjusted to the darkness and thus would not be able to see him.

"Greenaway," Raider said very softly.

The man stopped. He knew he was vulnerable, blind almost defenseless. "What do you want?"

"I'm a friend of Harry Jones," Raider said. "He sent me."

"Jesus, you frightened the shit out of me. I thought sure I'd been nailed by one of those fucking squatters. What does Harry want?"

Raider was tempted to shoot him on the spot. He knew the bastard deserved it and wouldn't give him a fighting chance if their positions were reversed. Raider really thought about it for a while.

"Hey, you still there?" the gunslinger asked. "Did you see Ella?"

Raider knew who Ella and the Greenaway Boys were from information telegraphed to Doc from Chicago.

"Yeah, I'm still here," Raider said. "You ever hear of a Pinkerton named Raider?"

The man laughed. "I hear that son of a bitch acts tough. I'd like to meet him sometime."

"You just have."

"What?"

Raider could see the man searching the darkness for his form, peering in the direction from which his voice came. His night vision must be improving.

"I'll make you an offer," Raider said, "though you don't deserve one. Either throw your gunbelt on the ground now or walk with me down to those lights yonder where we can both see each other plain."

He thought about that. "My name is Walt. I can't throw my gun down, Raider. You'd put me in the jail and I'd hang for sure. I don't have no hankerin' to draw agin' you neither. The offer you're making me ain't no kind of offer to make to a man."

"It's all you'll get from me," Raider told him.

"I'll pay you with gold."

"I'll pay you back in lead."

Raider's steely voice indicated to Walt that their talking was done. He moved toward the area Raider had mentioned, where the lights from the cabin windows fairly lit up the street. It was no city streetlight, but enough for two men intent on killing each other to do what they had to do.

Walt went to one end of the well-lighted area and Raider to the other, facing each other about thirty yards apart. For the first time they got a good look at each other.

"You go ahead, Raider, reach for your gun when you're ready. If you left things to me, we'd both just forget about this for tonight and go our separate ways."

"You're quite a talker, ain't you?" Raider said. "Drop your gunbelt. I'm taking you in."

"No."

Raider went for his gun.

He whipped out the Remington .44, thinking about nothing in the world at all and allowing his whole mind to serve his gun hand and gun eye. It all happened too fast for his conscious mind to make decisions.

Raider was way faster than Walt. His first .44 slug caught him in the chest and set him stepping backward on his heels. His next bullet caught him in the gut and doubled him over. One in the shoulder or side spun him and knocked him in the dust. Raider emptied his gun into him and rolled him against a cabin wall with the force of the bullets.

One by one the lamps went out in the cabins. In half a minute this section of town was in utter dark and stillness. Raider could hear himself breathing.

"Ella is mad as hell over brother Walt getting hisself killed," Joe told the others. "She and Harry Jones rode here by dark and are staying in a deserted house not far from the Prospect ranch boundary. Harry has sent men to claim Walt's body from the marshal in Calistoga. Meantime Ella wants us to hit back hard at them Pinkertons. Not Raider, 'cause he'll be expecting us, but the two on the train. One is a Pinkerton and the other a company security man. I had them pointed out to me. You want to come, Zak?"

Joe and Zak rode south through the mountains and then came down into the foothills opposite Rutherford, well below the Prospect ranch and where no one would be looking for them. They waited for the down-valley train at Rutherford station. When it pulled in, Joe and Zak jumped aboard the first passenger coach. They left it at the next station down and tried the second. Joe spotted Paul Heron and Willie McPhee riding together.

He eased Zak into a seat quick so Heron and McPhee wouldn't notice them in particular.

"We been seen," Zak said. "I saw the look the thin one gave us, and he said something to the fat one, and then he looked at us too."

"That's just their railroad-cop behavior," Joe said. "We don't look like landowners or store clerks, so they give us a long hard look that's supposed to spook us. Don't worry about it. We got these two cold. We gonna pay them back for Walt getting killed."

"Yeah, we owe that to Walt," Zak agreed.

When the train was under way, they nodded to each other, drew their Colts, and ran down the aisle to take Heron and McPhee unawares. They were gone!

The two men looked under the seats, stalked down the coach, harassed the passengers, checked everything—till they saw the open door at the end. They figured McPhee and Heron had made their escape through it, until the two came at them from behind, guns drawn, from beneath the back seats.

Willie put a .45-caliber cylinder of lead in Joe's heart, and Joe went down on his knees, eyes staring, blood leaking from the sides of his mouth.

Paul was about to blast Zak with a sucker shot between the eyes when he tripped and fell. His gun rattled over the floorboards.

Zak turned on Willie an instant before Willie registered that Paul was not going to do his stuff. Zak fired, and the bullet creased Willie's left shoulder. Willie was near the door. He could have fired back or got his ass out of the way of Zak's next shot. Wisely he moved his ass, and the bullet whistled by a rabbit whisker clear of his ribs.

With all his jumping about, Willie could find no stance to shoot. So he kept jumping—right on out the open door of the moving train, with another of Zak's bullets chasing after him like a starved mosquito.

Paul raised his eyes to find himself staring into Zak's gun barrel.

"Git up so you can die like a man," Zak told him. "I want to see yer eyes when I pull the trigger."

Paul obligingly tried to stand, but his right ankle gave way beneath him and his face twisted in pain.

Zak laughed. "Sprain your ankle? It hurts? Good. It don't hurt half as much as this bullet will when you get it in the gut. I want you to have time to think before you die, time to regret messing with the Greenaway Boys." He looked down the coach at the other passengers, who had backed away as far as they could. "This don't concern none of you. Keep out of it and I'll leave you alone."

Paul reached inside his boot to massage his ankle. "I think I've broken it," he moaned.

"Won't matter to you where you're going," Zak cackled. "Up there they all got wings."

As Zak leveled his gun barrel on Paul, Paul squeezed the trigger of his boot gun and hot lead tore through the leather of his boot and pierced Zak's leathery skin.

Tom looked up from his meal with Vittoria. "I suppose it's ironical that Paul Heron should pretend to have a broken right ankle and Willie McPhee get a real broken right ankle in jumping off the train. Those guys are like me. We're just mere mortals when compared to Doc and Raider."

Vittoria said nothing.

The door to the dining room burst open and a woman rushed in, followed by the winery foreman. Tom had never seen her before. The foreman shrugged his shoulders, as if to say he would have had to hit her to stop her coming in. Tom nodded, and the man left. The strange woman seated herself beside Vittoria and spoke to Tom in a hoarse voice.

"I've had a lot of sadness in my family," she said. "I've just lost two brothers."

Tom, wondering who she was, thought maybe she had come because they had something in common. "I've lost two brothers as well, and a third is missing. Is that why you came to see me?"

"I couldn't give a shit about *your* brothers," the woman said and swallowed down Vittoria's glass of wine. "I came here to pay you off for killing mine."

She pulled out a little pistol and held it almost in Tom's face before she uttered a loud cry and twisted in on herself.

Vittoria's eyes were round with horror, her face was immobile with shock, and she held a steak knife dripping with bright red blood. The stout woman next to her dropped the gun on the table and fell off her chair.

"It must be Ella," Tom whispered, amazed. "You just killed Ella, Vittoria. You saved my life!"

He rose from his chair and clasped her to him. As he held her, his eye chanced upon the gun the woman had dropped on the table. A .22 Remington Elliot. He saw the owl eyes crudely carved in the wood handle and knew it was his brother Peter's gun.

The squatters were roused. The newspapers had it now that the railroad lawyers would be dealing fresh with a new Congress after the elections. Special mention was made of the valuable reports filed by Pinkerton agents on the scene, which were said to have instigated the new action. Hopes were high that old wrongs would now be righted. To annoy Doc, Raider claimed sole responsibility for the reports and was quoted at length on various things which he claimed not to remember when he sobered up.

Jones was a common name, and more than a few innocent men were threatened within an inch of their life in the Napa, even though they looked nothing like Harry, solely because their name was Jones. Finally one of Harry's men talked. He was caught with food and ammunition at four in the morning just south of St. Helena. He got a plain offer. Hanging straightaway by the vigilantes who caught him or five twenty-dollar gold pieces donated by Tom Crevetti and a safe passage to Napa City in exchange for hard information on Harry's whereabouts in the valley.

When a man is sitting on his horse past four in the morning, his hands bound behind his back, a lamp thrust in his face and its light glinting on gun barrels, and he sees someone uncoiling a length of rope and help is very far away—he decides to die silent and true or he just can't hardly be stopped talking.

It was still dark when the vigilantes roused Doc and Raider at the widow Jackson's. Tom was with them by then.

Tom said, "He's in the empty house just before the log cabin where Ernest got shot."

"He might have been there then, too," Doc said reflectively.

"You keep out of this one, Tom," Raider said. "The Napa is going to need Crevettis and is going to be depending on you. All you men, hang back. Doc and me will handle this one." In an undertone to Doc, he added, "I just can't stand to see any more of these fucking amateurs getting killed. With just you and me, we stand half a chance. Don't forget to bring your rolled-up newspaper, Doc."

To Raider's surprise Doc went back inside the house and reappeared with a rolled newspaper under his arm.

They walked right up to the lonely house in the predawn darkness. Doc unfurled the sheets of newspaper and methodically crumpled each one up. He inserted them beneath a corner of the ancient, tinder-dry building and lit them with a match. They had quite a long wait before the fire got seriously under way.

The smell of smoke set one of the two remaining Greenaway Boys to yelling. He charged out the front door into Raider's gun. He died like an unwanted varmint.

The second stuck his head out the window and lost the top of his skull to one of Raider's .44 bullets. He sagged lifelessly in the window of the burning building.

Was Harry there?

Flames lapped the house in a hungry conflagration before Harry Jones made a break for it. He came out with his arms raised above his head, his big Peacemaker in his right hand, aimed at the sky.

"I never knew you were such rough sons of bitches," he said with a grin to Raider. He winked at Doc, put the Peacemaker to his forehead, and ended the Jones empire.